PRAISE FOR MIA HOPKINS
AND HER BOOKS

"Mia Hopkins knows how to put characters on a page."
—*Heroes and Heartbreakers*

"Beautifully descriptive...hot, sexy and full of yearning!"
—*Delilah Devlin, bestselling author*

"Mia Hopkins is an imaginative author who doesn't take the easy road to a formulaic book."
—*USA TODAY*

"Off the charts hot."
—*The Romance Studio*

"And those sex scenes...Holy hotness!"
—*Crystal Blogs Books*

"Sweet and filthy at the same time, just the way I like it. This book made me so happy."
—*Read All the Romance*

"I absolutely adored every inch of this book."
—*The Romance Reviews, Top Pick*

COWBOY RESURRECTION

A COWBOY COCKTAIL BOOK

Mia Hopkins

Little Stone Press
LOS ANGELES

Edited by Jennifer Haymore
Cover by Syneca

Cowboy Resurrection/ Mia Hopkins. -- 1st ed.
ISBN-10:
0-9979922-8-X
ISBN-13:
978-0-9979922-8-1

To Manjinder Singh Sidhu, for your kindness, time and wisdom. Thank you for sharing your light.

To Jennifer Haymore, for believing in Monica and Dean. Thank you for continuing on this journey with me.

To Sienna Snow, for your generosity and valuable insight.

To Rachel, my fellow adventurer and partner in crime. I'm so lucky to call you a friend.

To my husband, Brent, for being my human Thundershirt. I love you.

And most of all...to every girl whose bullish heart refuses to follow the rules. This one's for you.

CHAPTER ONE

The Princess

Fall in love, embrace restlessness.

—PUNJABI PROVERB

Monica's father's voice was calm. "All we're saying is, it can't hurt to meet him, can it?"

"I don't know, Papa. You know I'm leaving in three months."

In the background, her mother's voice rose sharply. "He's studying to be a urologist at Stanford. Did you tell her that? He'll be right in her area when she moves back to Cupertino."

"*Soniye*, please calm down." Monica's father turned back to the phone. "Did you hear her?"

"Yes, I heard. A urologist." Monica withheld her sigh. "I guess you could give him my number. Tell him to call me."

"Okay, good." Her father lowered his voice. "That should satisfy your mother for now."

Monica smiled. "Thanks, Papa. I've got to go."

"See you at dinnertime, *beti*."

Monica ended the call as she exited the pitted highway. Putting her mother's matchmaking obsession out of her mind, she pulled onto the brand-new blacktop parking lot in front of the Silver Spur. It was still April but already the thermometer in the dashboard of her Prius showed 89 degrees. Two big, dusty pickup trucks took up spaces in the lot. She parked next to them and glanced at her watch. Eleven o'clock.

They sure start drinking early in Oleander.

She opened her car door and desert air flooded the air-conditioned interior. When she took off her suit jacket, the hot wind whipped through her sleeveless silk blouse, pulling the sweat from the surface of her skin and messing up the clips that held her long, wild black hair in place. Monica removed the clips, slung her tote bag over her shoulder and took a deep breath.

You're getting them on your side, one by one. Just do what you do best. He's just another cowboy. Nothing different about him at all.

Tension gathered in Monica's shoulders. She could pep talk herself all she wanted, but she knew the truth.

Dean MacKinnon was not just another cowboy.

Her phone buzzed. She pulled it out of her purse and checked the message.

Are you coming? He's here right now with his brother, but I don't know for how long.

She grinned. The bar owner, Tom Shelton, had had her back ever since she proposed her idea to him back in January.

I'm outside, she texted back. She slipped the phone back into her purse. Her high heels were silent over the hot asphalt as she made her way to the door.

The cool interior of the Silver Spur smelled like new paint and lemon wood polish, not a scent Monica equated with old small-town honky-tonks. Tom stood at the register tallying up some tabs while a pretty woman with red hair sat opposite him at the bar, highlighting passages in a big textbook.

Tom looked up when he saw Monica. "Good. You're here." He lifted the counter of the bar and stepped out. He had a gravelly voice and lots of tattoos. "Monica, meet my girlfriend, Wanda. Wanda, honey, this is the mastermind behind Oleander Rodeo Days."

Wanda's eyes lit up as they shook hands. "Oh, man. Tom won't shut up about you. Says you're doing something awesome for the town."

Monica smiled. "Some see it that way. Others..." She trailed off and scanned the room. At one of the corner tables sat two big men in cowboy hats, chatting quietly and watching a baseball game on TV.

"So he hasn't returned your calls?" Tom asked.

"No," Monica said. "Well, not the last five, anyway."

"I'll introduce you. Don't worry, MacKinnons don't bite."

"That's not what I've heard," Wanda said, raising her eyebrows at Tom.

"You hush, troublemaker." Tom gave his girlfriend a crooked grin before he started across the barroom. Ever since he'd taken over, the Spur had flourished. He was one of the rodeo's first sponsors—a godsend.

Tom brought her over to the table. "'Scuse me, fellas."

The brothers turned around, saw her, and on cue, both of them stood up at once.

Oh, my God.

Monica tried not to gasp out loud, but that was the reaction her body had at being confronted with a pair of giant, handsome men. Both were tanned and a little dusty, dressed in jeans, boots and long-sleeve button-down shirts. Clark was the taller brother, but buff and bearded Dean looked even hotter than the photos Monica had seen of him online. She could smell them where she stood and guessed they'd been working all morning. Warm leather, aftershave, dirt, skin, sweat. In a current state of extended celibacy, her body stood up and said howdy.

"Guys, this is Monica Kaur," said Tom. "Her family just took over the Rambling Ranch Inn. She's on the board of directors for the Oleander Rodeo Association. Monica, meet Clark and Dean. Their family runs MacKinnon Ranch."

The cowboys tipped their hats, but Dean shot an annoyed glance at Tom.

"Nice to meet you both," she said. "Call me Monica."

"Come join us," said Clark. He pulled out a seat for her, and she sat down. "We're watching the D-backs get whupped. You follow baseball?"

"I'm a Giants fan," said Monica. Clark grumbled good-naturedly, took his seat and turned his attention back to the game. They all knew the one she really wanted to talk to was Dean.

Tom cleared some empty beer glasses, gave Monica a conspiratorial wink and left. Monica leaned toward Dean to keep her voice down under the game.

"You're a hard one to get ahold of," she said cheerfully.

He narrowed his bright blue eyes at her and took a sip of beer. His hand on the pint glass was enormous. "We've already had this conversation over the phone. The answer's still no."

"One no and five unreturned phone calls? It'd take a lot more than that to run me off, Mr. MacKinnon."

Clark turned around and waved his hand. "Naw, none of that mister stuff. Call him Dean. Or Uncle Frowny Face. That's what our nieces and nephew call him."

Monica wasn't sure if having Clark's assistance was a good or a bad thing. On one hand, it helped to have an ally. On the other, Dean was looking more annoyed by the second.

"Before you tell me yes or no," she said, reaching into her tote bag, "just let me show you what we have planned." She pulled out her tablet and loaded the website one of her friends from Berkeley had designed for the rodeo association. It was clean, professional and modern. "Here's our home page. And our schedule. Here's where visitors can buy tickets. Take a look."

Monica walked Dean through the website, just as she had for dozens of people before him. Rodeo performances on Friday, Saturday and Sunday. A parade down Main Street. A rodeo dance. The crowning of a rodeo queen.

Dean said nothing, just sat there with his beer in his hand looking blankly at the screen. Clark lost interest in the game and kept his eyes glued on her tablet.

"What do you have lined up for the performances?" Clark asked.

She opened the link. "Bareback riding, barrel racing, ladies' breakaway roping, saddle bronc riding, steer wrestling, tie-down roping, team roping and bull riding, of course." She'd given herself a crash course on all of the events, courtesy of the Internet. "Finals on Sunday, with cash prizes."

"Who's sponsoring?" Clark asked.

"Tom got me Los Angeles Nightlife Group, plus his alcohol distributor and Tioga Beer. We've got the local radio station, the TV station and the *Oleander Oracle*. A dozen local businesses are all doing their part: Johnson Saddlery, the Chevy dealership, a couple of ranches, a couple of farms. It helps that all the proceeds go to the Oleander Fire Department."

"Not all proceeds," said Dean at last. Caught in his icy stare, Monica thought briefly about the videos of him she'd watched online. He regularly stared down 1,800-pound bulls and never flinched.

"What do you mean by that?" she asked, keeping her voice calm and even.

"I mean, Oleander Rodeo Days was your idea, wasn't it? What's your angle?"

"No angle, Mr. MacKinnon. Just bringing business to a town that needs it."

"And a motel that needs more guests, maybe?" He put down his empty glass.

"Who wouldn't mind a little extra business?" She smiled brightly. *Uncle Frowny Face, indeed.*

"It's a half-baked idea," he said flatly. "You've got Oleander Rodeo Days scheduled in a tight window between two major rodeos in the Central Valley. Both are professional shows that draw big crowds. Your local competitors are going to save up their time and money for one or the other, not for some amateur show in some Podunk town."

Before Monica could respond, Clark piped up. "Jeez, lighten up, Dean."

"Just callin' it as I see it." He shrugged and leveled his eyes on her.

Monica pressed her lips together. Why did that gaze have to be so direct? Up close his eyes were an extraordinary shade of blue, like swimming pools in the desert. Dean's arm was pressed against hers. She felt his hot, hard biceps through the thin cotton of his shirt. Suddenly she wondered what it would be like to run her hands over his bare arms, to touch his muscles and all those scars she knew he was hiding under his clothes.

She blinked and concentrated on the conversation at hand. "Everything you're saying is true," she said, "which is why I need you." She powered down her tablet. "Make an appearance at this event. Let us put your name on the marquee. It'd be a really wonderful draw for attendees. You're a local legend."

A crease formed between his eyebrows and he looked disgusted, as if he'd just stepped in a fresh cow patty. Monica quickly realized such a trivial thing as bullshit wouldn't bother a man like him, but the expression on his face told her he was about to turn her down.

She spoke before he could. "Before you tell me yes or no," she said again, "I'd like to show you the arena and get your take on it. As someone who's seen hundreds of rodeo venues. Please. You're an expert. I'd like to know your thoughts."

"You know, this is just a lunch break for us," he said. "We're heading back—"

"Go with her, Dean," said Clark. "I'm gonna watch a few more innings anyway."

Dean said, "But—"

"We'll catch up this afternoon," said Clark, waving his hand. "You two take your time."

Still not allowing Dean to say a word, Monica stood up. "And the inn is not far from here."

Clark watched his brother with an expectant face. Outnumbered, Dean grimaced one more time, pushed his chair back and stood up. "Fine," he said to her. "But you're driving, princess."

It was her turn to grimace. "Right this way, Mr. MacKinnon."

Dean said nothing as he followed her out the door.

* * *

Monica looked at the scowling cowboy out of the corner of her eye as her car slid silently down the highway. She didn't turn on the radio. She figured he wouldn't like the kind of music she liked, pop rock and Top 40. She definitely didn't like country music. Too much twang. Too much heartache.

At least Dean looked as uncomfortable as she felt. For one thing, he was too big for the car. He shifted in his seat and ground dark soil into her immaculate floor mats with the heels of his dusty cowboy boots. She could still smell him. Dirty cowboy, but not unpleasant—in fact, pretty far from unpleasant. Monica tried to ignore the quivery feeling in her stomach. Months without sex left her jumpy. She'd have to find some private time with her battery-operated buddy to take the edge off soon.

"So when did your family take over the Rambling Ranch Inn?" Dean asked. His soft, deep voice rumbled like thunder in the quiet interior.

"About a year ago. My brother bought it, actually. The family helps out. I came out about three months ago to do my part."

"Where are you all from?"

"From here."

"No, I meant originally."

She frowned. "Originally...here."

"Okay, what about your parents?"

"They're from here too." She glanced at him. He looked even more uncomfortable, so she cut him some slack. "My grandfather moved to Merced from India in 1919. He was a farm laborer. He and my grandmother saved money to buy a parcel of land right outside Oleander. My family's been farming it ever since."

"Grapes?"

She nodded.

"Like the Singh family?"

"The Singh family *is* my family."

"But your last name is Kaur. Are you married?" His blue eyes flashed over her fingers on the wheel.

She gripped the wheel self-consciously. No ring—as if she needed a reminder. "No, I'm single," she said. "Sikh women adopt the name Kaur."

"Why?"

"You're full of questions, aren't you?" She exited the highway and took the road leading to the Rambling Ranch Inn.

"Only 'cuz I prefer to be full of answers."

Monica said nothing. She wasn't in the mood to explain what Kaur meant. He'd probably make fun of her.

He reached down and adjusted his seat so that he could lean back and stretch out his long legs. "All right. So here's another question for you: why the hell would your family choose this place to get into the hotel business?"

The Rambling Ranch Inn had gone up for auction and Monica's impulsive brother, Ravinder, had put in a bid. She was still living in Berkeley when she'd found out the news. She was furious. Her parents had borrowed against the farm to buy the motel and the thousand acres it sat on.

"It's an investment for us," she told Dean, the anger still twisting in her gut. "We're trying to diversify."

He nodded slowly. "If it were me, I'd tear it down and farm it."

Her thoughts exactly. But Ravinder had been adamant. He'd convinced their parents to sink even more money into replacing the derelict plumbing system and refurbishing the rooms. She'd shown them the numbers, but they refused to listen. To her mother and father, Ravinder had a dream and they were willing to support it. It didn't matter that she was the one with a degree in marketing and a master's in business.

"We're taking a chance," she said, doing her best to hide her true feelings. "Trying something different."

She drove past the inn and turned onto a wide paved road. Parallel to the road ran a long row of eucalyptus trees. A hot breeze stirred their branches. The sun was high overhead and the trees cast no shadows on the pale gray asphalt. Monica turned off the air conditioner and lowered her window. The sweet, medicinal scent of eucalyptus filled the car. Trees from faraway, planted here. She wondered briefly if they ever felt out of place.

"Was this rodeo arena ever in use when you were younger?" she asked.

He shook his head. "Not that I remember. The folks who used to own the motel had a daughter who was a barrel racer. That was a long time ago, though. Before my time, anyway."

From her clandestine research, Monica knew that Dean was turning thirty-six this year. He was only four years older than her, but he gave off the jaded calm of a much older man.

"And no one ever used this arena for anything else?" she asked.

"Oh, I don't know. It's out of the way, I guess."

"Out of the way?"

"When I was in high school, people used to drive out here and make out in their cars. A kind of lovers' lane." He paused. "Yeah. That's what we used it for."

The thought of a young Dean MacKinnon rutting a cheerleader in a pickup truck gave Monica an unexpected thrill. "How about you? Did ever you come out here?"

"Well, ain't you full of questions." He smirked at her.

At the end of the windbreak was a wide dirt field studded with patches of tall weeds. The weeds were so

happy to grow unmolested, they'd burst into flower—
yellow, white, gold. The rusted white gates of the old
rodeo arena stood lonesome, the bleached bones of a giant animal that'd died in the desert a long time ago.

Monica turned off the engine and they got out of the
car. The hot, unrelenting wind whipped at her again;
her unbound hair blew back and she swept it off her face,
annoyed at how wild and unruly it always was. Dean
pulled down the brim of his cowboy hat. She looked
down. Tangled among the weeds were dusty, crushed
beer cans and shreds of desert-eaten litter.

"Let's see what you've got here," Dean said.

She followed him toward the arena, struggling to
keep her balance over the pitted, uneven dirt. Patent
leather heels had been a bad choice, but she soldiered on,
determined to keep the aloof cowboy's interest.

"Who's producing the show?" he asked.

"We signed Miller-Davis Pro Rodeo," she said
proudly. It had been a slog just to get the famous pro-
duction company's attention. They kept reminding her
again and again that they hardly ever bothered with
amateur events.

Instead of being impressed, Dean said nothing.

She frowned. "What's wrong with Miller-Davis?"

He shrugged. "Nothin'. They do an all right job."

"All right? What do you mean by all right?" She
stopped walking. "You've got something to say, Mr.

MacKinnon, I think you should say it. I—we—have got a lot riding on this show."

"You signed on the dotted line. Nothing I say's gonna change that."

"But—"

He stopped and turned around. "They've got a couple of dinks, is all."

"Dinks?"

"Bulls that don't buck." Dean turned back to the ring. "You want rank bulls. I know a stock contractor not far from here that might could help you out. I'll give him a call."

Monica smiled to herself. This was exactly why she needed Dean MacKinnon on her side. "I'd appreciate that," she said, watching her footing. The weedy ground was more uneven by the rusted barriers. Dean looked at everything with keen eyes as Monica stood by.

"So what do you think?" she asked.

"Classic eight-event rodeo? Regulation arena with a return, which you've got here." He grabbed hold of the metal bars and gave them a shake. Monica saw his forearms flex as he gripped the metal. "These are rusted out. Not sound. You're going to need new posts and panels. Wouldn't be safe for the livestock or your visitors otherwise." He tipped his hat back slightly to look at the rest of the arena. "Stock pens back there, bucking chutes here, roping chutes over there." He rubbed his chin and nodded. "Seating?"

"Aluminum bleachers. We rented them."

"They'd go there." He gestured with his hand toward the opposite side of the arena. "And you need arena lighting for the nighttime events." Dean walked the perimeter of the rusted-out fencing while Monica stumbled behind him, trying to keep her balance. "It's a good piece of land," he said. "Easy to find from the highway. Lots of parking for horse trailers and campers. You'll need to clear a big space for a turnaround. You thinking about concessions?"

"Three aisles of booths behind the bleachers. All local vendors. A Tioga Beer garden too."

"All right." He nodded again to himself. "Okay."

The made a slow circuit around the arena. The sun beat down on them. Dean looked perfectly comfortable in the heat, but Monica was baking in her silk shirt and linen suit skirt. He took a quick look at her and very subtly led her around the curve of the arena to a stand of eucalyptus trees. They stood in the shade for a second so that she could rest.

Dean hooked his thumbs into his belt loops and leaned against a tree. "Pains me to say it, but I think you've got something here."

"I like to think so. With your help, we'll be able accomplish much more. It'd be volunteer work, but all of us are volunteers." Monica wiped her forehead with the back of her hand. "Can I ask you a question?"

"Shoot."

"How did you become a professional bullfighter anyway?"

"Long story or short story?"

It wasn't a chore to listen to Dean MacKinnon talk, and she was enjoying the shade. "Long story."

"When I was a kid, my dad took us to all the local rodeo events in the Central Valley. If we could get out there in a day, he'd drive us. I remember sitting in the stands with him, watching everything—the bulldoggers, the roping, the bull riding. My brothers all loved the bull riders. But I was different. I always liked the bullfighters. Back then we called them rodeo clowns."

"Did they do the same things you do now?"

"Sort of. Rodeo clowns wore face paint and dove into barrels and told jokes to the crowd. But every time a rider got himself into a fix, the rodeo clown was there. He put himself between the bull and the rider. His job was to make sure the rider had that extra second he needed just to get away. These days the job's split in two. The barrel man's the entertainer. The bullfighters are the ones who protect the riders."

"Do you have bulls on your family's ranch?"

"Sure. Beef bulls. Little different, though." He kicked at the dust with the toe of his boot. "When I got a little older, my father got me a job with his friend, name of Bo Walker. Bo was a bull rider, retired. Back then he was dead set on becoming known as the breeder of the rankest bulls on the West Coast. I worked his stock weekends and summers. Soon he had me handling the bulls. He taught me a lot. I began doing local rodeos as a bullfighter. Got a reputation, I guess. I learned from the guys around me and just worked my way up. Bit by bit."

"Bull by bull." She sat down on a fallen tree. Its trunk was smooth, worn away by the elements. "Aren't you ever afraid?"

To her surprise, Dean sat down next to her. "Afraid? Naw. Excited, more like." He paused. He had his own flavor of drawl, the accent of a man who was from a lot of places but nowhere in particular. "Fear's no good. You won't be in the right frame of mind to do the job. Someone could get hurt—you, or the rider, or one of the other bullfighters. You can't be afraid."

Monica looked at him. As he spoke about his work, his whole demeanor changed. He relaxed into his body. He unfolded his arms and the rigidity melted out of his shoulders. God help her, he looked even hotter, if that were possible.

"So you're saying that when you are in the ring facing down a furious one-ton bucking bull, you're not afraid at all?" she asked.

He gave her a half-smile that doubled his good looks. "Okay, maybe a little." He leaned back on his arms and looked out onto the ghostly arena in front of them. "The riders—some of them do it for grins, I suppose. But they're athletes. And they're chasing eight, looking for a payday. Me? The other bullfighters? We're there to do a job. We can't let ourselves be affected by fear, even if we feel it. Fear leads to mistakes. And mistakes like that—they've got a high price."

Monica studied his face. Even though he was at rest, his eyes were alert and watchful. From how he talked about his work, she knew he was proud of it. She could identify with him on that point. Her work was important to her too.

"So what's your story?" he asked. "I heard the Singhs' daughter went away a long time ago. Became one of them fancy college kids, more degrees than a thermometer. Working out in Silicon Valley, getting richer'n Steve Jobs. That true?"

Monica always wondered if anyone in town talked about her. People in the Sikh community sure did—she was "that old maid", still unmarried at thirty-two. "The Silicon Valley part is true," she said, "but I'm not a computer person. I'm in marketing. I help tech start-ups establish their brand and spread the word about their products."

He nodded slowly. "How about the rich part? Is that true?"

"It's good money. But richer than Steve Jobs? No. Not quite."

"So Oleander Rodeo Days is just a little jewel in your crown?"

She snorted. If only he knew the financial trouble her family was in, that joke wouldn't seem so funny. She reached down and brushed the dust from her patent-leather heels. "Yeah. A very little, very dusty jewel."

"Are you moving here for good?"

She shook her head. "No. Once Rodeo Days are done, I'm hightailing it back to Cupertino. How about you?"

He shrugged. "Not sure yet."

They chatted for a little while in the shade. To her surprise, Dean told her a little about his family and what it was like growing up on a ranch. Talking to him was easier than she'd thought.

When she had cooled down at last, Dean stood up and offered her his big hand. She took it, but when he pulled her up, her heel caught in a gopher hole and she stumbled forward, face-planting into his broad, rigid chest.

"Careful," he said softly. With sure, swift movements, he hooked one arm around her waist and rested his other hand flat against her back, helping her gain her center of balance at once. She wavered a little bit, but his stance was solid, as though his legs were rooted in the earth like trees. Her skirt had ridden up just a little and she was straddling his thigh. Sudden heat flared up wherever her body was touching his—her chest, her back, her waist, her hands. A powerful, greedy ache grabbed hold of her between her legs. She didn't move. Neither did he.

"Miss Kaur," he whispered. "Are you all right?"

They were standing so close together that Monica could see the faint brown freckles on his cheeks, the crinkles that formed at the corners of his blue eyes when he smiled.

"Call me Monica," she said.

"Monica," he murmured, "are you all right?" His mouth, framed by that short, dark beard, was wide and luscious, as tempting to her as an oasis in the heat.

Monica wasn't a fool. She'd watched videos of him in the ring. Dressed in his gear and cowboy hat, Dean was fast as a cat and completely fearless, putting himself between angry bulls and fallen riders again and again and again. In the most famous incident, a rider had gotten hung up in his rope and Dean had taken a hoof to the femur while cutting the man free. Dean was fearless.

His local legend went back much further. Back in high school, he'd been Oleander's very own cowboy Casanova, a football player and weekend bullfighter more handsome than a movie star. Some of the women who'd known him in school had told her stories about him that had left her blushing. When he'd gotten married, they'd cried enough tears to fill the aqueduct. Mystery shrouded his eventual divorce. Monica couldn't dig up the dirt, even though she'd tried.

And there were dozens of fan sites dedicated to the hotness of Dean MacKinnon. From *Dean's Queens*, a group of gay cowboys in San Francisco, to *Jailbait No More*, a small army of young women who showed up at his events wearing T-shirts that said *Hey, Dean, I'm Finally 18*. Dean MacKinnon lived in an all-you-can-eat buffet of willing sexual partners.

Up close, Monica saw the truth. Those fans weren't wrong. The man was a bona-fide sex god.

He grinned as though he could read her mind. "Are you all right, princess?"

Temporary insanity was her only excuse. Months without sex, and her body was like a bull bucking in its chute. No brain. No logic. No words. All go.

"Don't...call me that," she whispered, staring at his mouth.

She leaned forward, tipped her head and, eyes open, pressed her lips against his.

He kept his hypnotic eyes open too, blue as the desert sky above them. Against all sense his mouth was cool, as soothing as a drink of cold water on a blazing-hot day.

The handsome bastard stood as still as a statue. Shame tingled in her fingers and toes, but Monica was so deep under his spell that for once she didn't care. She pressed her palms flat against his chest and realized he was just as muscular as he looked. His body was like stone, but hot and alive. She slid her fingers over his curving chest muscles. Through his shirt, his soft mat of chest hair crinkled against her touch. Her toes curled in her shoes.

Still he didn't move, letting her explore him. His lips tasted slightly bitter from the beer he'd been drinking at the Silver Spur. She was perched on her tiptoes, the balls of her feet digging into the grit as she pushed her body forward, trying to get a response out of him.

He gave her nothing. Nothing but that curious blue gaze, burning into her.

Finally, too mortified to keep going, she pulled away.

God, what is wrong with me? On top of being too horny to live, she was now too ashamed to look him in the eye. She lowered her hands and stepped back away from him.

"Excuse me, Mr. MacKinnon," she said, her voice suddenly raspy. She cleared her throat and licked her lips. They tasted like him. "I don't know what came over me. I'm sorry. I...misunderstood."

She'd already taken two steps toward the car when he reached out and encircled her wrist in his big hand. His hold was neither gentle nor hard. With his other hand, he slowly reached up and touched her cheek. Monica froze. His palm was calloused. She blinked and looked up into his eyes. His pupils were wide, and for the first time, she realized he was breathing as hard as she was.

"First of all, call me Dean. And no," he said softly, "you didn't misunderstand."

She swallowed. Something about him made her unhinged. Like the rules of behavior didn't apply when she was close to him. "It's just that...since I've been home...I've been..." *Lonely.* She trailed off, unable to say the word.

He stroked her cheekbone with the knuckle of his index finger then slid his hand behind her neck. The simple move steadied her. "It's all right."

And then she was back in his arms. He ran his fingers through her hair and rested his fingertips against the burning bare skin on her neck.

"I'm gonna kiss you back now," he whispered. "You okay with that?"

She couldn't speak. She nodded.

He closed his eyes at last and kissed her. He pushed his bottom lip against the corner of her mouth, and when her lips parted, he swept the inside of her lips with his tongue, a soft lick that drew a soft sound from her throat, halfway between a moan and a sigh.

Dean put one hand on her waist and one hand behind her head, bending her backward like a bow. Monica had nowhere to go, nothing to do but take it all.

Overwhelmed, she reached up and grasped Dean's flexed shoulder with her left hand. Her right arm was crushed between his rock-hard chest and her own wildly beating heart.

In her hometown, she was a spinster, an unmarried girl who gave her mother no shortage of heartache. But the cold, hard truth was also Monica's biggest secret. Since her train wreck of an engagement, one-night stands were her preferred way to blow off steam back in the Bay Area. No questions, no expectations. Just quick, dirty sex behind closed doors. And in the morning, a kiss or two goodbye before a clean getaway.

None of her hookups had ever kissed her like *this*.

Through gaps in her mental haze, Monica noticed details about Dean MacKinnon's technique. Passionate but precise. Curious but unhurried. His kiss was a perfect melding of heat and friction. With just a kiss, he summoned the rising tide of her lust, a sweet, hot rush of blood infusing her body like liquid fire.

He pulled away just enough to whisper, "More?"

She closed her eyes. "Yes."

In the shade of the brim of his cowboy hat, he kissed her again.

Hints of aftershave lingered at the edges of his well-groomed beard. Bay rum, old-fashioned and spicy. The scent got its hooks into her and wouldn't let go. When she moaned, Dean bit her lower lip gently.

Damn, she thought. *He is good.*

After fourteen years, she'd returned to her hometown nothing more than an outsider, disconnected from her family and her faith. For the last three months, she'd had to pretend to be something she wasn't, something purer and better, caught between worlds like some kind of ghost.

But here and now, she was no ghost. Dean MacKinnon was solid, and he was here, and he was holding her. His kiss obliterated all her worries. With his big arms around her, she felt grounded for the first time in a long time.

His hand, rough as uncut granite, massaged the back of her neck as he slowly explored her mouth with his lips and tongue. He was so strong and calm that his power fed her, and her fluttering spirit alighted in him, hungry for his steadiness.

Dean gently pushed the tip of his tongue between her parted teeth and gave her a sweet, tentative lick. When she licked him back, she felt his grip on her tighten. She dug her fingers into the cotton of his shirt. His body was hard all over, nothing but skin stretched over muscle.

Time passed in heartbeats and quickened breaths until panic bubbled up from some tight place in Monica's chest. She pulled away.

"Are you all right?" he asked.

No. Her mind began racing again. *Absolutely not all right. My family is less than a mile away, a hive of cousins and aunties and uncles, a mom who is hell-bent on finding me a proper Sikh husband, and a father who wouldn't think twice about running you over with a minivan.*

Dean grazed her jaw with his thumb. "What's wrong?"

She shook her head as she looked down at his chest crushed against hers. *You. You big* gora. *You're all wrong. Tall and hot and white and Christian and completely, totally, unforgivably wrong.* She was furious at the ungovernable urges of her body. How could she let him affect her this way? Back in the Bay Area, she could do whatever—and whomever—she wanted. No one was watching. Here? Everyone was watching. When it came to a fling with Dean MacKinnon, Monica knew she had to call it what it was.

"This is a mistake," she whispered.

He kept his hold on her. "You want it and I want it. How is that a mistake?"

"Trust me. It is."

"We're adults. Free souls in a free goddamned country."

She licked her lips again and looked up at him. "It's not that simple."

For a moment, he searched her face with his remarkable eyes. "You have obligations. I can't fault you for that," he said softly. "But it'd be fun. Monica, it'd be a hell of a good time." He lowered his lips to her ear. "I could see it in your eyes the moment you walked into the Silver Spur. I can feel it rising off you now."

She closed her eyes again as his warm breath washed over her skin. "What?"

"You're a woman in need of lovin'. I could help you with that. I'd love you up good."

The man was a beast. Her eyes fluttered open. "I've heard about you."

"Rumors are rumors." He paused. "I'd take care of you, though. Then you'd see."

"See what?"

"If the rumors are true." He waggled his eyebrows at her, and she smiled in spite of the loopy way he made her feel.

"Tell you what," he said, "you and me, we're going to work together, that's for sure. I want to help you with the rodeo." When he stroked her cheek, his fingertips pressed lightly against her jaw. "But I want us to play together too. You're not planning on staying and neither am I. So no strings attached. How's that grab you? Can I spend some time convincing you?"

He'd read her mind aloud.

"Let me…let me think about it," she said quietly.

He nodded.

They shared one last slow-simmering kiss before he let her go. Without a word, they walked back to her Prius. Monica's legs were shaking as she drove them down the highway to MacKinnon Ranch. She didn't trust herself to speak.

When she exited the highway, he caught her looking at him, but he didn't say anything, just smirked behind his hand as he rubbed his beard.

Cocky bastard.

She drove through the open gates of MacKinnon Ranch and down to the small compound of buildings at the end of the driveway. No one was around.

Dean leaned forward, tipped his head and kissed her cheek. A quick peck, but still her body throbbed at the contact. She wanted more—more touching, more kissing, more secrets, more Dean.

She willed her voice not to tremble. "Are you free tomorrow?"

"What do you need?"

You. More of you. "I need your help reviewing the contracts and streamlining the association's list of action items."

"'Action items', huh?" Another smirk. "All right. Tomorrow at eleven. The diner."

He got out of the car, shut the door and went inside the big house without looking back.

* * *

Monica could barely keep their names straight.

First was Aphra, the knockout blonde who worked at the hair salon and came into the diner for a cup of coffee before dropping her toddler son off at daycare. Percy was the pretty, older hippie, a local masseuse and physical therapist who sold essential oils and crystals at the farmers' market. Heather was the mayor's trophy wife, a Kim Basinger lookalike from Massachusetts who had somehow ended up in a dusty California cow town. Then there was Demi, the stone-faced but beautiful widowed wife of a local farmer who now managed operations on her own. She came in with her friends Addison, a CPA who looked and dressed like a naughty librarian, and Andrea, the equine vet tech from Oklahoma, a willowy girl with long, dark braids.

Each one stopped at the booth where Monica and Dean worked, an endless parade of salivating women. And each one looked at Dean like he was today's blue-plate special. He'd introduce each one to Monica, and then they'd start on their schtick.

First the windup.

"Long time no see," they all said in their own way, smiling flirtatiously. "You're looking good, Dean. Yeah, things are going well. You know, same old, same old." Then they'd drop their voices. "How's your dad doing? Oh, I'm so glad he's better. Tell your mother I said hello. She's such a strong woman." They'd take a subtle step forward, shifting their weight from one foot to the other. "You know..."

And then the pitch.

"My sister's in town this weekend and she'll be watching Tyler. You and me should grab a cup of coffee." Or, "Is your leg still bothering you? I could take a look at it again, if you wanted." Or, "Harvey's on another hunting trip this week. It gets *so* boring at home by myself!" Or, "I'll be out on the lake with some girlfriends next Wednesday if you're not busy. They'd love to meet you. They're big bull riding fans." Or, simply, "Call me. Let's catch up."

When the last woman walked out of the diner, Dean looked at Monica and raised his eyebrows. "What?"

She shook her head slowly. "I didn't say anything."

"No, but you were thinking it."

"They're *my* thoughts. I don't have to tell you anything." She pursed her lips and met his gaze. His eyes were full of silent laughter. Curiosity got the better of her. "Did you really sleep with all those women?" she whispered. "Is that what that was all about?"

"Is that what you think?"

"Did you?"

"How do I say this without being rude?" He smiled and took a sip of coffee. "I don't have to tell you anything."

She frowned at him.

The lunch crowd was in full swing by the time Monica and Dean finished up their paperwork. Dean ordered a burger and Monica ordered a chicken salad sandwich. While they waited for their food, Monica put all her papers and contracts away, turned off her tablet and tucked it into her tote bag. She thought again of all those women, all seeking him out for what would probably be another dynamite roll in the hay.

"Must be nice," she mumbled.

"What?"

"Having your business out in the open like that without worrying about what other people think about you."

"What business?" he asked. "All those women did was say hello."

"Yes, but it was the *way* they said hello. I have a mind to ask the waitress for a mop and a wet floor sign to put next to the table."

He laughed at that. "For the record, they came to me. I didn't call them over." As he studied her face, heat rose in her cheeks. She fought to keep her expression neutral. "You know," he said, "not worrying about what other people think isn't a God-given gift. It's a conscious choice. You can make it too."

Monica shook her head. "Actually, no, I can't. Just sitting here with you, a white man, by myself—that's already pushing boundaries. Even if it's for work." She leaned back and studied the room. Familiar faces, but all strangers. "Being back home makes me feel...I don't know. Like too many people are watching me. I just want to hide."

Their food came. Dean doused his fries with ketchup and offered some to her. She took a couple. Then she took a couple more.

"Sometimes I feel the same way," he admitted, to her surprise. "I haven't stayed in one place this long since...I can't remember when." He paused. "My father, he's gone through this two times in the past. He's got lots of fight in him yet, but he's not as young as he used to be. And each relapse—it takes its toll."

As he spoke, Monica regretted complaining about feeling stifled. A mother who spent her time on dating websites trying to find her daughter a husband was nothing compared to having a sick parent. Monica didn't know if she had the strength or emotional maturity to cope with something like that.

Deflated by guilt, she asked in a softer voice, "So when it gets to be overwhelming, what do you do to relax?" When he waggled his eyebrows at her, she rolled her eyes and said, "I mean, besides *that*."

"To blow off steam? I work on the ranch. There's never a shortage of things to do. But to relax?" He wiped his mouth with a paper napkin. "Riding is always good. And my brothers and me, we lift weights, try to outdo each other."

Monica had to admit that that particular hobby was paying out good dividends. "How many brothers have you got anyway?" Anywhere she went in Oleander, she seemed to run into a big, buff MacKinnon brother.

"Three," said Dean. "I'm the oldest. Daniel's number two. Clark—you met Clark—he's number three. And last is Caleb. My baby brother. He's twenty-two."

"That's a big age difference between you two."

He shrugged. "We call him *Oops* behind his back. Among other things."

She took a big bite of her sandwich. It was tasty. "So riding and lifting. Is that it?"

"Let's see. Um, my sister-in-law's got a huge library in the house. It's great, 'cuz I like to read."

"You?" she asked. "You like to read?"

"That surprise you?" He smiled. "We're not all illiterate Okies, you know. We don't spend all our time shootin' rats at the dump."

She raised an eyebrow at him.

He hesitated. "Okay, maybe after we shoot rats at the dump, we pick up a book or two."

She laughed and stole another fry from his plate.

"I got into the habit on the road," Dean continued. "A book's easy to carry. It's cheap, and TV only turns my gears so far. I guess I needed more. Much more." He paused and looked at her across the table. The seats of the booth were upholstered in robin's-egg vinyl that set off the blue fire in his eyes. He'd hung his hat on the hat rack. His dark, disheveled hair and neatly trimmed dark beard only made his eyes look more feral. Monica had to look down at her half-eaten sandwich to keep from falling into his gaze as though it were a deep well or a high cliff next to the ocean.

Someone should post a sign on his forehead. "Danger. Falling women."

"You know something else I like to do out here?" he said at last. "Go for drives."

"Around Oleander? What's there to see?" she scoffed. "Burnt grass? Dust storms? Roadkill?"

He pointed a french fry at her. "Okay, Miss Snooty-pants, this ain't the Bay Area. No ocean, no fog. But we have our own secret spots." He chomped on the fry as he watched her face. "In fact, let's go for a drive after lunch."

"This afternoon?" She glanced at her watch. "I've got another meeting at three. I shouldn't—"

"Don't worry. The place I want to take you—it's not far."

* * *

"Turn here," Dean said.

After a twenty-minute drive down the highway, he directed her down an old fire road that wound around a blond, dry hill of grass. The road was unpaved but wide and well maintained. There was nothing out here but scorched grass and an occasional gnarled oak, dwarfed by the lack of water, providing small spots of shade in the blazing midday heat.

"Keep going," he said.

They turned around the bend and on the western-facing side of one of the hills, the dry grass was carpeted in bright orange, as if someone had spilled cans of paint across the landscape.

"This is the spot."

She gasped. "What is this? Did someone plant this?"

He shook his head. "Wildflowers. They grow on their own."

"Why here?"

"It's cooler on this slope."

"What kinds of flowers are they?"

"California poppies."

She stopped the car in the middle of the road and they walked out. The riotous color grabbed her eyes and wouldn't let go. Everything dulled in comparison to that vivid orange. The dry grasses that just a moment ago seemed so yellow had turned a dull straw color. Even the clear blue sky appeared grayer.

Only Dean MacKinnon's eyes stood out, those pools of cool, pure blue. He looked at her to see if she liked what he was showing her.

"Beautiful," she said quietly. She walked gingerly through the field of flowers. "How did you find this place?"

"The flowers grow here every year. Even dry years. We used to ride horses all up and down these hills. Never paid much mind to whose property was whose, although we probably should have."

"Bet you brought a couple of girls up here to impress them," she said.

He said nothing but followed her out into the middle of the field until they were surrounded by poppies. The color deadened her other senses, and when Dean leaned over to kiss her neck, she jumped in surprise.

"Shh." Dean reached down and picked a poppy from the thick carpet at their feet. With surprising delicacy, he tucked it behind her ear and brushed the hair away from her neck and shoulders. He gazed at her a moment like a man admiring his handiwork. The blossom was warm and velvety against her skin.

She looked up into his eyes, and her lust rose in response to the heat she saw there. She stepped forward and rested her hands on his rock-hard shoulders. Without a word, he put his arms around her and kissed her. Full lips, wicked tongue. Her hands slid down around his curving triceps. He was solid, bull-like—a thick, handsome man and a dynamite kisser. Monica was so turned on, she didn't trust herself to speak when Dean pulled back.

"So," he whispered against her lips. "What do you want?"

"I don't know." Her voice was barely audible, a ghost of air carried away by the wind.

"I think you know." He kissed her again, and before she knew what was happening, he'd pulled her down to the ground with him. The dry grass and soft blanket of flowers crinkled like hot paper beneath them. He sat down and she straddled him, her knees crushing petals that looked like orange fire in the desert.

Dean took off his hat, placed it on the ground, and traced a trail of hot kisses down the side of her neck. Pleasure ran a circuit through her body, firing her nerve endings as her lust rose to high tide.

She dug her hands through his dark hair. It was silky, long enough to curl. When he began to lay hot, open-mouthed kisses on her throat, she grabbed his hair in her fingers and tugged at it gently. A low moan rumbled in his chest.

His lips found hers again. They quickly established a rhythm of breath and tongues that pulled all conscious-ness from her brain. She was flying, far too high on Dean to realize she was riding him, rubbing herself against the hardening bulge in his jeans.

He broke their kiss and rested his forehead against hers. He let go of her waist and dragged his fingers through her hair, clasping it and gently pulling it back until her lips parted with a gasp.

"Tell me what you want." His deep voice sent shivers up her spine.

She was silent, paralyzed with pleasure.

"Tell me what you want, Monica," he said again. His firm tone made her insides clench. Already she could feel how wet she was, how ready.

"You need it. Same as I do." He touched her face and skimmed his fingertips down her throat. "Don't you?"

"I do." She was still. "But no one can know about this."

"I understand."

"Dean, I'm serious. Not a soul. Promise me."

He nodded. "I promise."

In a heartbeat, he lifted her and laid her gently on her back. She closed her eyes. Peach-colored sunlight shone through her closed eyelids. Dean distracted her with hard kisses as he undressed her, pulling her blouse from her skirt and undoing her buttons, one by one. He pulled her up, unhooked her bra clasp and whipped the bra off her. Wind cut through the ravine, stirring the grasses and flowers and racing over her skin, making her nipples harden. Dean cupped her breasts with his enormous hands and stroked her nipples with his fingertips.

"Beautiful," he said quietly.

He kissed her mouth once more, a deep, commanding kiss that made her blood bolt to her pussy like quicksilver. Still rubbing her nipples with the pads of his fingers, he traced an achingly slow trail of kisses down her chest and stomach until he reached her belly button. He brushed his fingers in a line between her hipbones, and she almost jumped out of her skin.

She opened her eyes as he sat up and stripped off his shirt.

"I don't have anything with me," he said, looking down at her. "But...I can still make you feel good."

Monica stared at Dean's naked chest. She couldn't have imagined a hotter sight if she tried. Broad as a door, he was tan and tight and beautiful. Well-built shoulders sloped down to rounded pectoral muscles and abs packed together like six shiny apples in a gift box.

Her eyes raked over him. Random scars marred his skin, silvery stripes, wide jagged slashes and puckered lines where stitches had been put in and taken out. Dark hair covered his chest, narrowing into a trail that led down past his shallow belly button until it disappeared behind the shiny buckle of his belt. The name *Cecilia* was tattooed over his heart, the ink faded to slate green. A second tattoo covered his right biceps, ornate knots and spidery lines.

"You all right?" He slid his hand across his abs, as if he needed to draw any more of her attention to his body.

"Who's Cecilia?" she asked.

"My mom."

God, how many women had ogled him like this? Did he enjoy seeing the looks on their faces when he took off his clothes? Did he even care anymore?

Monica cared. The sight of a shirtless Dean MacKinnon had already burned itself into her memory. She'd remember it until she was an old lady in her rocking chair.

That one time I had me a cowboy, she'd think to herself. *A long time ago.*

She glanced down past his belt buckle. Over the last couple of weeks working with real cowboys, she'd noticed that they wore their jeans a little looser to be able to move as they worked. Dean's were the same, but there was no concealing the big bulge behind his fly. He saw where she was looking and smiled as he rubbed it with his palm.

He dropped to his knees, grabbed his shirt and spread it out on the ground. Gently, he helped her onto it. With his big hands, he gathered her skirt up over her hips until it bunched around her waist. She was wearing a plain cotton thong, but he looked at her with appreciation twinkling in his bright blue eyes.

Without another word, he embraced her. He smelled musky and sexy. She savored the weight of him, pressing her into the earth, crushing the flowers. As he kissed her neck, she ran her hands up his muscled back, her fingertips grazing his hot skin in lazy trails.

He hooked his thumbs into the elastic of her underwear. "Up," he murmured.

She raised her hips as he slid her panties off.

"Spread your legs," he said.

The edge of command in Dean's voice made her drip hotly onto his shirt. Staring at his face, she parted her thighs and leaned back on her elbows to watch him as he lay down between her legs.

Dean didn't touch or tease her. He didn't stroke her legs or skin or play with her breasts.

He simply lowered his head and kissed her, long and hard, sealing his lips over her sex. She yowled in surprise and tried to clamp her legs shut, but he held them open with his enormous hands, and she was pinned to the ground, unable to move.

And then he went to work.

His hot tongue began to lap languidly at her, up one side of her pussy and down the other, teasing her open. He placed his big thumbs on her outer lips and spread her gently. Her entire body felt raw and exposed, and when he dipped his tongue inside her, she gasped and jumped reflexively, like a knee hit with a tiny hammer, every nerve on high alert.

For a long time, he pleasured her, making her wetter and wetter with each masterful lash of his tongue. Soon she was drifting above the poppy field, high on the opiate of her own arousal.

Just when she thought she couldn't fly any higher, Dean lifted his head and swiped her clit with the hardened tip of his tongue.

Pleasure sliced through her. She gasped and squirmed again. His hands clamped down on her legs, pinning her to the dirt. He pressed his lips against the front of her pussy and began to strum her swollen clit with his tongue. He didn't stop, his unrelenting rhythm jacking up the orgasm that was threatening to break inside her like a thunderstorm.

His lips, his tongue, the sensation of his beard against the hypersensitive skin of her inner thighs, the feel of his calloused hands gripping her open, the way he knew exactly what he was doing—Monica's body tightened like a windup toy. No one had ever turned her crank like Dean. She was so wet. When a new rush of moisture trickled out of her, Dean growled and quickened the pace, a man on a mission to see her fall apart.

She was sweating and cursing quietly. The sun beat down on her. There were flowers tangled in her hair. Dean pushed his body forward and nestled his rock-hard shoulders behind her knees. With one last trick up his sleeve, he opened her legs wider, pushing her thighs up and out until she was completely open, like he was cracking the spine of a brand-new book.

At exactly the same time, he pressed his tongue against her clit, hard.

The orgasm exploded out of her, a pent-up monster finally let out into the light of day.

Ecstasy crushed her in long, agonizing waves. She convulsed as he held her steady, his tongue never leaving her, his grip never loosening.

After the last tremors of her orgasm slid through her, Monica lay perfectly still on the ground. The hot sun burned her, and the wind licked the sweat from her skin. As hot pleasure drained out of her, she concentrated on catching her breath, dry desert air filling her lungs.

Dean rested his bearded cheek on her thigh and stroked her hips with a surprisingly light touch. A few seconds passed before she realized she'd reached out and torn handfuls of flowers out of the earth as she'd come. The velvety orange petals were crushed in her fists. She unclenched her hands and the petals blew free.

She sat up slowly and reached for him. He brought himself to his knees and let her kiss him, slowly, graciously, as though they had been lovers for a long time. When she broke the kiss, he lifted her chin with his forefinger and looked into her eyes.

"Why so lonely, princess?" he whispered.

She stroked his sun-warmed shoulders and said nothing.

* * *

When Monica finally caught her breath, Dean stood and helped her up. He still had a massive hard-on. She reached for him once more. While she kissed him, she slid her hand down those rock-hard abs and over the hot metal of his big brass buckle. But he took her wrist before she was able to go any lower.

"Today was for you," he said softly. "All for you."

"What the hell?" she blurted out. "That's weird."

His eyes crinkled up and he laughed through his nose. He brought her hand to his lips and kissed it. "Make sure you know what you want. I ain't in no hurry."

She stared at him, bewildered, as she buttoned herself up. He picked up his shirt, shook it out and put it back on. He tucked it in and adjusted his belt.

"Ready to go?" he asked.

They drove past the Rambling Ranch Inn without a word. Monica was sunburned, breathless and guilty. One of her aunties was watering the begonias outside the front office. Monica leaned down in her seat, afraid that what she and Dean had just done was written all over her face.

Oh God. What have I done? This was no anonymous motel hook-up in San Francisco. This was Dean MacKinnon, the most famous man in town. If her family found out what she was up to—Monica shuddered. *This is bad.*

"You okay?" he asked. He'd put a poppy in his hatband when she wasn't looking. The little orange blossom flickered like a flame.

"I'm fine," she lied.

When they reached the parking lot of the diner, most of the patrons were gone. Dean's ancient pickup truck was one of the few cars left in the lot. She pulled into the empty space next to it to let him out.

After she put the car in park, he turned to her. "You should come with me when I visit Bo Walker this week. See the property, check out the bulls."

She nodded. "Let me check my schedule. I'll let you know."

They looked at each other in silence. Dean was completely clean and put-together. What they'd done in the field could've been a feverish daydream or a product of her wishful imagination. But then she caught sight of the flower in his hatband and the still-raging bulge behind his fly. She pressed her thighs together and felt the slickness he'd left between her legs.

The urge to kiss him was so strong, she had to grip the steering wheel to keep from acting on it. There were patrons standing at the entrance of the diner. A couple passersby ambled along the sidewalk.

Dean opened the passenger door. "I think we're going to enjoy working together. What do you think?" He turned, touched the brim of his hat and gave her a small nod. "Miss Kaur," he said, his eyes searing hers.

"Mr. MacKinnon."

He closed her door, got into his truck and started up the engine. As he drove away, Monica sat in the silent interior of her car and listened to the jacked-up beating of her heart.

CHAPTER TWO

The Clown

Breaking even is ending up in purgatory as far as I can tell.

—TOWNES VAN ZANDT

A mop of dark curly hair appeared on the other side of the breakfast table. A tiny hand gripped the back of the chair. The chair rocked precariously as Dean's monkey of a nephew swung into place for breakfast.

"Morning," Dean said.

"Good morning, Uncle Dean." The little boy was neat and clean, all dressed for kindergarten. Georgia, Derek's mother, came in from the kitchen and put a pancake on her son's plate.

"Here you go, kiddo. Pancake, Dean?" Georgia asked. She held a skillet full of pancakes in one hand and a spatula in the other. The new baby was due in a few weeks, but she looked like she was going to pop any minute.

"I'm good, thanks." Dean finished reading the newspaper, folded all the sections neatly and straightened the pile. He took a sip of his second cup of coffee.

"Where's Grandpa? Where's Grandma Cece?" asked Derek.

"They took a trip to the hospital in Bakersfield with your Uncle Caleb. They'll be back this afternoon." Dean opened the syrup bottle and poured a little puddle on Derek's pancake. "Say when."

The little boy stared at the growing puddle and said nothing.

"You gonna eat the whole bottle?" Dean asked.

The boy looked up at him with a mischievous twinkle in his eye. Dean smiled and snapped the bottle closed. "Little monkey."

Daniel opened the back door, walked into the kitchen and hugged Georgia from behind as she stood by the kitchen sink. "Hey, sweetheart," he murmured, kissing the back of her neck. He rested his hand on her pregnant belly. Together they closed their eyes, smiling, and stood still, a moment of tenderness in the swirl of another morning.

A sudden rush of longing flooded Dean's chest. Quickly, he looked down at his coffee cup, annoyed at himself for intruding on his brother's privacy.

At the table, his other brother Clark took a huge bite of pancakes and dripped syrup onto the newspaper as he read the business page. "So where are you going today?" he asked, his mouth full.

Dean cleared his throat. "Bo Walker's. Going to see if we can get some bulls for Rodeo Days."

"You taking that girl? What was her name, the one on the rodeo association?"

"Monica Kaur. Yeah. She wants to see them." He hadn't stopped thinking about her in the last two days. When she finally called him last night, he'd perked up like a teenage girl whose crush was on the phone. Didn't matter that all she'd talked was business.

"She's hot stuff," said Clark with a grin. "She single? Seeing anyone?"

Dean put down his coffee cup, trying to sound non-chalant even though against all logic, Clark's words made him see red. "Ask her yourself, you're so interested."

Daniel came into the dining room with his breakfast and sat down. "Say hi to old Bo for me, will you? Tell him we all saw Dandelion Wine buck off Bruno Silva on TV last weekend. That sure was something."

"I'll tell him." Dean said.

Daniel turned to the little boy. "Go brush your teeth and get your book bag. I'm taking you to school today."

Derek the monkey swung out of his chair. There was a smear of sticky pancake syrup on his cheek. "Okay, Daddy."

* * *

Three months.

Dean had been home three months and already he felt like he was drowning. The facelessness of each moment bled into the next. He could feel himself growing older and softer and slower with each passing day.

When he was working the circuit, it was easy to keep bad feelings at bay. He was always moving, never giving himself enough time to stagnate.

And it felt good to start over in a new town every couple of days. Like he'd been erased. Newly baptized, almost a different man, no longer subject to the old misapprehensions or regrets of the past.

On the ranch, at least the work was good and honest, and Dean liked seeing his efforts tallied up each day by feet of fence restrung or number of calves vaccinated or square miles of pasture reseeded or leveled. He didn't mind that he was answering to his younger brothers. In his absence, Daniel and Clark had become competent cattlemen, as skilled if not sharper than their old man.

Dean clenched his jaw.

The old man.

Their father was the whole reason he and Caleb had come back home, the whole reason Daniel couldn't sleep at night and Clark spent most nights at the Silver Spur. The old man's cancer had come back with a vengeance, and the whole family was here to rally around him, to support him and help him fight off the disease one more time.

The show producers called Dean regularly. Was he coming back? When? How many shows? Could they put him on the schedule?

"Not yet," was all Dean could say. "Just keep me in mind. I can't give you an answer yet."

What kind of answer could he possibly give them? His father was dying, even though no one would say it aloud. He wouldn't be able to do any shows until...the inevitable.

He loved his family. Good people, every single one.

And yet Dean wished he were back on the road. Anywhere but here, where bad memories and new melancholy were eating him alive.

He hoped the trip out to see Bo would be good for him. He borrowed Caleb's truck. His baby brother's Silverado wasn't much to look at but the kid took good care of it. When he took the exit, Dean clenched the steering wheel just a little tighter and put on his sunglasses. Too many women in town who were hungry for a piece of him, and not in a good way. He hoped they'd mistake him for Caleb.

As promised, Monica stood just outside the fire station waiting for him. Her long black hair was gathered in a simple ponytail, and he could see the smooth, dark nape of her neck. She was dressed in another silk blouse, dark jeans and the silliest pink slippers he'd ever seen. The jeans showed off her wide hips and the curve of her round ass. In his mouth, his tongue twitched. For a split second, he thought he could still taste her, the sweet, rich flavor of her sex burned like a brand into his senses.

He stopped the truck at the curb, got out and opened the door for her.

"I told you to dress down, for Chrissakes," he said by way of hello. "It's a ranch."

"I *am* dressed down," she said, taking the hand he offered and climbing up into the cab of the lifted truck.

Dean couldn't help admiring the view. The woman had curves like a dangerous mountain road. A flashback of her surrounded by orange flowers, half-naked and coming hard beneath him, made the rest of his mind go momentarily blank.

"You all right?" she asked as she put on her seat belt.

He blinked. "Yeah," he said curtly. He shut the door.

The drive to Walker Ranch took an hour and a half. Dean kept his hands on the wheel and tried to keep cool. Monica messed with her tablet computer and chattered about her plans for Oleander Rodeo Days. Who was involved. Who was doing what. What was happening when. She went on and on. Dean's mind was wandering back to the taste of her smooth brown skin when she asked him a question at last.

"Huh?" he said.

She lowered her sunglasses and raised an eyebrow at him. "I said, did you work with Bo Walker when you were in high school?"

Dean cleared his throat. "Uh, yeah. My first job."

She tapped something into her computer. "Bo Walker owns Dandelion Wine? Isn't that—"

"The three-time world-champion bull?" Dean nodded. "Bo grew up with my dad. Won a lot of awards as a bull rider before he went off to Vietnam. When he came back, he retired from riding to become a stock contractor. He started with one bucking bull and two good cows. Now he's got sixty, seventy bulls on his property. Maybe a dozen horses he's training for roping and pickup."

"That's impressive. When's the last time you saw him?"

"Three, four months ago. Back in St. Louis, I think." He turned onto the winding road that led up to Lake Isabella.

She turned off her tablet and slipped it into her bag. "So what's it like, not moving around the country like a pinball?"

It's hell. "It's fine," he said. Tightly wound and moodier than usual, he had no desire to be psychoanalyzed today. He decided to turn the focus on her. "How about you? What made you move away from here in the first place?"

"Nothing dramatic. I got into Berkeley, and after four years, Northern California just grew on me, I guess. Most of the companies I want to work with are up there, so it's a logical place for me to live." She looked out the window.

Her answer wasn't as deep as he wanted it to be, so he pressed her. "I knew kids in high school who were itching to get out of Oleander. Were you trying to get away from your family?"

"No, not really." She gave him a sideways glance. "Not at first, anyway."

"What do you mean?"

"I guess for this to make sense, you have to understand that my family is very big, very tight-knit."

Had she forgotten who she was talking to? You couldn't swing a dead possum 'round these parts without hitting a MacKinnon. "Yeah. I think I get that."

"Also, I was raised in a very traditional way, going to the temple, praying twice a day. My father, my brother, all my uncles—they wear turbans and they don't cut their beards."

He nodded. "I've seen the Singhs in town before. Good men, all business owners and farmers."

"My fiancé was a Sikh. We met at Berkeley." She paused. "His family lives in Stockton. When our engagement ended, we caused a minor scandal. Especially when he got married just a few months later."

So she'd been burned before, just like he had. "Did that bother you?" Dean asked.

"Not as much as I thought it would. But my family?" She shook her head. "Very bothered. Very, *very* bothered. Now my mother is obsessed with seeing me married. It was easy enough to avoid her when I was up north. But here? Impossible to escape." Monica sighed and looked up at him. "Is Walker Ranch much farther?"

Dean glanced back at her. His picture of her was becoming clearer, but she was still a puzzle. One he wanted to solve. "Naw. We'll be there soon."

* * *

As Bo took them on a UTV tour of his ranch, Dean watched Monica work. She was as perceptive and sharp as a gypsy horse trader, but she hid her true self behind a wall of charm and a smile that could light up a moonless night. Old Bo had no idea what hit him. Before he knew it, Bo had offered up half his stock and told Monica he'd call the rodeo producers himself to make all the arrangements. They shook hands and in a hot minute, Bo was beaming and opening up his finest bottle of bourbon on the front porch while Monica held out her empty glass.

She had gone to rinse her slippers off with a garden hose when Bo leaned over to Dean and said quietly, "That one's a keeper."

Dean took a sip of the Pappy Van Winkle he knew Bo wouldn't have opened for him if he'd come alone. "I'm not interested in keepin' anyone at this point, Bo."

The old cowboy frowned. His thick, white eyebrows came down with the corners of his mouth. "Bullshit, boy. I see how you look at her."

"You're imagining things, old man. I just met her."

"Never stopped you before." Bo drained his glass and let out a happy hiss. "And for the love of God, stop calling me 'old man'."

Back in the truck, Monica didn't allow herself one minute of gloating before she turned on her computer again and checked off more items on her list. "Good. That took about as long as I anticipated. That leaves me enough time to pop by the sheriff's station to approve all the sponsors' signage before it goes off to the printer's."

Dean shook his head as he started up the engine. "My God, woman."

"What?"

"Don't you ever give it a rest?"

"The sooner this all gets done, the sooner I free up my schedule for the rest of the stuff that's going to land on my plate soon," she explained without looking up. "If it sits, things just get worse. I don't want to get behind."

"It's a rodeo *association* isn't it? What about your associates?"

She shrugged. "They've got their own tasks to handle. These are mine."

"I know everyone on that board," Dean said. "They're nice people, but I wouldn't exactly call them go-getters. You're doing more than your fair share. I know it."

"Well, if you want something done right...yadda, yadda." She waved her hand absently.

He looked at his watch. "It's eleven. What time do your signs need to be at the printer's?"

"Before they close at five."

He left Bo Walker's property and headed north. "All right. I'm taking you somewhere."

Monica looked at him at last. "What?"

"You ever been up to Lake Isabella?"

"Yes."

"How many times?"

She paused. "A couple."

He smiled. "Don't lie."

"Okay, once."

"How old were you?"

"Six," she said sheepishly. "It was a school trip. Polli-wogs."

"Then you're long overdue."

"Dean—"

"You said it yourself. Printer at five."

"But I have to work."

"This *is* work. Market research. Think about it. Lake Isabella or Rodeo Days. Most townspeople that weekend are going to be at one or the other." He grinned. "Best know your competition, right?"

She turned off her computer and looked at him with an impatient sigh. "Fine. An hour. No more."

* * *

After stopping at the bait shop for a six-pack, Dean drove around the shore of Lake Isabella and headed up into Sequoia National Forest. The road narrowed into a mountain highway and, though it had been years since he'd come up here, Dean followed it to the unmarked turnoff he and his brothers had discovered when they were in high school. The forest grew lusher and thicker around them.

"I'm taking you to a super-secret spot. Just before the Kern River feeds into the lake. MacKinnon Rock." Dean could still see Monica's suspicious expression through the lightly mirrored lenses of her sunglasses. "Well, I call it that anyway," he added.

In a cloud of dust, Dean parked the truck by the side of the road in the shade of a black walnut tree. He grabbed the six-pack and a couple blankets out of the truck bed. Monica climbed out and shut her door.

"Follow me," he said. "Watch your step."

They walked through a break in the underbrush and the Kern River appeared before them, dark and beautiful. As far as Dean knew, only he and his brothers ever visited this swimming hole. A large boulder created a break in the current where a smaller creek flowed into the river. The water was clear and deep.

"Pretty, right?" he said.

"Not too shabby," Monica replied, but she was smiling. She sat down on a granite slab and hugged her knees.

"There's lots of secret spots up and down the river." He paused. "You know, I always liked living out here. It's the memories that make me want to turn tail." Dean walked up to the edge of the river and nestled the six-pack in the water to keep it cool. Then he began to undress.

"What are you doing?" Monica asked, taking off her sunglasses.

"Going for a swim."

"Are you crazy? That water is freezing."

"Hot day like this?" As he took off his hat, he looked up at the blazing sun directly above their heads. "Come on. It'll feel good. Take off your clothes."

She shook her head. "No way. Go ahead. I'm staying here."

"No, you ain't. I'm gonna toss you in one way or another." He took off his shirt. "You decide if it's clothed or naked."

"The hell you are." Her voice rose a notch above the soft tumble of the water. "I'm not getting naked here. What if someone sees?"

"Someone? A lizard? A bird?" He laughed as he removed his boots and socks. "I'll protect you, Monica. Just leave your clothes on that rock. Your panties will be nice and warm when it's time to get dressed again."

She held up a finger and waggled it at him. "No. No way."

"Come on. Ain't you never gone swimming naked before? And you grew up out here?" He took off his shirt. "You oughtta be ashamed of yourself."

She was trying not to stare at his chest and failing miserably. "Sorry," she said. "I must've been studying for my SATs."

He undid his belt buckle and took off his pants and underwear all at once. The sunlight warmed his bare skin. He turned and pointed at her. "All right. I gave you a chance." He started toward her.

She crab-walked backward up the rock and scrambled to her feet. "No! Dean, don't you dare!"

"Hairy naked redneck coming at me? I'd do what he says."

She held up a fist. "I will punch you in the goddamn balls, Dean MacKinnon. This is a silk blouse."

He couldn't help himself. He started laughing. "Then take it off, princess." He took another step toward her and she started to dance, jumping from one foot to the next. She looked so cute that he stopped in his tracks. His laughter faded away.

"Monica," he said softly. "Princess, look at that pretty river. Come on. One time. With me. What do you say?"

With a wary expression, she looked at him, then at the river, then back at him again. "I don't like...I don't like mud between my toes," she murmured.

"I'll carry you."

She frowned. "Fine," she said at last.

Dean watched her undress. First she stepped out of her slippers. Then she removed her jewelry and slipped it into the pocket of her blouse. She unbuttoned the blouse and carefully laid it on the stone. With a sigh, she removed her belt and jeans. Still wearing her simple black bra and panties, she took a moment to tie up her hair.

With her arms above her head, Monica looked like a fantasy come to life. Smooth dark brown skin, full breasts, wide hips, small waist. Dean stared. His eyes couldn't get their fill. Blood rushed through his system like a river swollen with snowmelt. His cock twitched and hardened.

She looked him in the eye, clearly avoiding looking at anything south of his belly button. "Why do we have to be...naked?" she said. "Why can't I just wear my underwear?"

"Dyes and detergents, princess. Can't contaminate the water. Think of the environment." He grinned. It was a bald-faced lie. But the image of her naked body had haunted his dreams for two nights straight. He had to see her again.

With another sigh, she unhooked her bra. "Turn around," she said.

"What? Why?"

"Just turn around. I'll climb on your back."

"My back? Why don't—"

"Do it, MacKinnon!" she snapped.

He put up his hands and turned toward the river. "Okay, okay."

His ears strained to hear the sound of cotton sliding on skin as she took off her bra and panties. His hard-on began to ache. He heard her quiet footsteps on the rock as she came close.

"Now get down," she said softly.

He got down on his good knee, and she wrapped her arms around his shoulders. She pressed her smooth, heavy breasts against his back. He reached behind him and hooked his hands behind her thighs. The sensation of her sweet, soft sex nestled up against the small of his back was almost enough to make his knees buckle beneath him.

The tally was three. He'd jacked off three breathless, frantic times since the incident in the field. A fully grown man who'd had enough sex for ten lifetimes wasn't supposed to react to anything this way. And yet Monica Kaur had gotten under his skin in a way he couldn't explain.

"You ready?" he asked. His voice was rough.

She rested her chin in the crook of his neck and shoulder. "I guess so," she said glumly. Her breath caressed his ear. His hard dick jutted out at an acute angle, casting a funny shadow on the rock. Carefully, he walked into the water. His old injuries—dozens of them—began to ache. He pushed the pain aside.

"It's cold," he warned her. "Really cold."

"Whose idea was this again?" She tightened her grip on him. Goose bumps rose on her arms in anticipation. When the water came up over his hips and over her shins, she hissed and wiggled like a snake. Dean enjoyed the reaction.

As he waded out into the middle of the river, the river rocks on the bottom became smaller until he stood on a bed of pebbles. The sound of rushing water grew louder.

"There's no mud here," he said. "Do you want to get down?"

"Okay," she said.

Before she could loosen her grip, he leaned backward and dunked them both in the river over their heads. The frigid water felt like an electric shock and Dean popped up, breathless, pushing the hair out of his eyes and whooping with laughter.

"You asshole!" Monica yelled, but she was laughing too, splashing him with great sheets of icy water. Her hairdo had come loose and her black hair streamed down over her shoulders like rivulets of ink. It was the sexiest thing he'd ever seen.

He didn't remember reaching for her. But all of a sudden she had thrown herself into his arms and they were kissing like crazy teenagers again, lips and tongues exploring, eyes wide open with wonder. The sound of the river filled his ears along with the kick-drum beat of his own heart. Monica had a hunger that mirrored his own. She cupped the back of his neck with her hands, and pulled him deeper into the kiss. Only then did they close their eyes and give in, collapsing into each other like two stars going supernova at the same time.

Heat supplanted cold. His blood was boiling so hot in his veins, he couldn't even feel the frigid water anymore. Too lust-addled to be graceful about it, Dean picked her up again and carried her awkwardly back to the river-bank, almost losing his footing on the stones. As carefully as he could, he laid her out on the rock and kissed her, over and over again until she was breathless. He kissed her neck and the hollow at her throat. He kissed a trail down her sternum, then took one dark nipple between his lips and suckled her hard. She arched against him, digging her fingernails into his forearms. With his other hand he reached down between her legs. He swiped his fingers against her. She was slick and hot.

"Have you been thinking about me?" he whispered against her breast. He began to stroke her with his fingertips. The soft lips of her sex began to swell; her clit was like a hard seed against the pad of his thumb.

She nodded and gasped. "For two days straight. I can't stop."

"I can't stop thinking about you either."

Too revved up to go slow, he plunged a finger into her and stroked the front wall of her impossibly tight pussy. He lowered his lips to her clit and began to tongue it without mercy. The taste of her fed a deep hunger inside of him that had been growling for days.

His cock needed her. Now. But in order for this to work, she had to come first, and she had to come hard.

If Dean MacKinnon had learned anything after ten years of soul-numbing debauchery, it was how to make a woman come fast and hard.

Whimpering, Monica lay paralyzed on her back as Dean jacked up the tension in her body. Soon, she was shaking against him, struggling to hold back her orgasm. His tongue was relentless on her tender clit. Her rosy pussy quivered around his finger; carefully but quickly he slid another one in, stretching her. He began to thrust gently, back and forth into her slickness, trying to get her used to the sensation. She was small. It was going to be a tight fit. As he opened her up with his fingers, he loved her up with his tongue. Her entire body was trembling.

"Dean, I'm close." Her hoarse whisper drove him wild.

He flicked his tongue quickly against her stiff little clit, back and forth, again and again. Her wetness amplified the sound of his tongue and his fingers working away at her. He drowned in his frantic need to have her, to feel her around him, to explode.

She grabbed his shoulders and sat up halfway. She squeezed her eyes tight and bit her lip and whimpered once, just once, before he felt her body break loose.

"Oh, fuck, yes." She threw her head back and moaned.

Her entire lower body convulsed, once, twice, three times. The slick muscles in her pussy contracted hard, crushing his fingers like a nutcracker. Her pretty nipples tightened, and goose bumps covered her whole body. She was so wet with arousal that a fresh puddle formed on the granite under her ass.

Still shuddering, she collapsed back onto the rock as Dean carefully withdrew his fingers and brought them to his mouth. He licked them as she watched him.

"I missed how you taste," he said softly.

She blushed hard.

He reached across to his jeans and pulled out a condom. Without fanfare, he tore the packet open with his teeth and rolled it on as she stared.

"You're huge," she said.

"That's why you had to come first." He knelt down and carefully flipped her onto her belly. "This way hurts less. I promise."

Parting her legs with his knee, he straddled her left thigh and, from behind, nudged her hot, slick opening.

"Come up on your side a little," he said softly.

She lifted her right shoulder and planted her hand against the warm stone.

"There you go." He leaned down and kissed her neck. "Tell me to stop if it hurts too much, all right?"

"Okay."

"Promise me, Monica."

"I promise."

He slid his hips forward and seated himself between her sweet, round ass cheeks. Still dripping from her orgasm, her pussy stretched to accommodate him as he pushed in the head of his cock, then half his shaft. The grip of her sex was amazing. Dean was breathing so hard he could barely get the next words out.

"Take two deep breaths. In and out. Twice."

On her second inhalation, he thrust hard, pushing himself as far as he could. She didn't flinch or whimper. Instead, she arched her back and thrust her ass out toward him as if to offer him more. The gesture made his balls tingle. She liked sex—just like he did.

He stroked her ass cheeks and gave them a gentle squeeze. "You all right?"

"Yes." She licked her lips and arched her back even deeper.

He wondered if she'd flinch at dirty talk. "You ready for me to fuck you now, Monica?"

She didn't flinch, but she did do something that made him lose his mind. She squeezed his shaft hard. He heard a soft kiss as the lips of her sex tightened around the base of his cock.

"Yes," she said, closing her eyes. "I'm ready."

Blood on fire, he rested one hand on the rock and one hand on her hip. Dragging himself out of the grip of her pussy, he pulled out halfway and then thrust forward hard, slamming into her ass and making it jiggle. They grunted in tandem, two animals locked together by lust.

"Same rule," he murmured. "Tell me if I hurt you."

"I promise," she said again.

He found his angle quickly. With an unrelenting lust that burned in his bones, he fucked her, his abs slapping against her beautiful ass again and again and again. Lost in the pleasure of making love to Monica, he forgot about everything—the pain and awkwardness of being back home, the guilt at being a failed husband, the aching loneliness of the road. He was nothing but this, here and now, his dick in her pussy, the filthy, sexy sound of two people crashing into one another and uncovering something profoundly good.

Then she surprised him once more. She reached behind her and stroked his face. A moment of tenderness in a wild storm of fucking.

"You're amazing," she said quietly. Her dark eyes narrowed and burned into his. "Dean. You're amazing."

He began to come, hard and long, and for a split second, he almost believed her.

* * *

Together, they lay naked in the sun on the blankets, drinking beer, talking and looking up at the cloudless sky.

"Your fiancé was a damn idiot," he said. "How long were you engaged?"

"Almost three years."

Dean whistled low. "Long time." He glanced over at her. Pain ghosted her expression for only a moment before it disappeared.

"He wasn't a bad guy. We had lots of issues, but in the end, we wanted different things. He wanted me to stay home and raise kids. I wanted to pursue my career first." She took another sip of beer, trying to find the right words. "He loved me, though—a different version of me."

"Then he didn't love *you*, princess."

"He wasn't a bad guy," she said again.

"No, he's a fucking dipshit. I find him, I'ma put a boot up his ass."

She laughed softly. "Crazy Okie."

"Proud of it too." He smiled. She was easy to talk to. He couldn't remember the last time he'd had a real conversation with a woman. "Tell me something. Your family...they wouldn't take to me coming around, would they?"

She shook her head. "They want me to marry a Sikh guy and start a family. According to them, I should've started a long, long time ago."

"And you? What do you want?"

A bright blue jay landed at the water's edge, took a drink and flew noisily into the trees. Monica watched it go. "Since I broke up with my ex, there's been no one serious. Mostly one-night stands—my mother would throw me off a cliff if she knew." She paused. "I guess if the right guy came along, I might consider getting married. But I try not to think about it."

He understood what she was saying. He'd put marriage out of his mind a long time ago. Been there, done that. Had the ugly-ass scars to prove it. "What else do you want?"

"I want to bail my family out," she said with a sigh. "The motel was a bad idea, but they're not letting go. The rodeo might help them at least break even, and if it becomes an annual event, they might even turn a profit in two or three years."

Dean nodded slowly. He'd gotten her all wrong. She wasn't self-involved. Just the opposite. She was taking care of her family.

With the back of his knuckle, he reached forward and stroked her arm from her shoulder to her wrist. "And what else do you want?"

When she smiled at him, he realized he wanted to be the kind of man who was worthy of a smile like that. "I have a job waiting for me in Silicon Valley," she said, leaning forward as though she were sharing a secret with him. "It's a start-up. I'd be director of marketing. It's a huge promotion. A big raise. The sooner I can get out there, the better."

"Sounds like you have everything planned out."

"They're keeping the job open for me. I'm planning to make my getaway right after the rodeo. After all the numbers are in." She looked at him. "What about you? Do you think you'll find your way back to the circuit?"

"Hard to say." He left it at that.

She frowned. "You know, the laconic-cowboy act is getting kind of tiresome. Does that work with most people?"

"Most *normal* people, sure," he said. "And I'm not trying to hide anything from you. Here. Let me prove it. Ask me anything."

The sly look in her eyes gave him pause. "Anything?"

He stuck to his guns. "Yup."

"Okay." She sat up and faced him. "How many women have you slept with?"

Shit. He took a sip of beer to gather his thoughts. "That's what you open with? Goddamn."

"You said to ask you anything." She raised her eyebrows. "Well?"

"Don't rush me." He dragged a hand through his still-damp hair. "Let's see. I'm kind of an old geezer now, and I started early, so you need to take that into account. Then I was with my ex-wife, four years, just her. After her, free-for-all. I've been slowing down in the last few years."

"You're stalling."

"That's 'cuz it's just a number," he said. "Doesn't mean good sex, for one."

"But you're a superstar. I thought you'd be able to skim off the cream of the crop."

He shrugged. "Depends on what you mean by 'good sex'. And where you are in your life when you need it."

With a wicked grin, she reached forward and stroked his chest and abs. Her hands lingered on his scars. "So what's good sex to you?" she asked.

"This." He raked his eyes up and down her naked body. "This is some damn fine sex."

"Be serious."

"I *am* serious." He lay back down and put his hands behind his head. It was easier to say some things when he wasn't looking directly at her. "Some days...I wake up. I can't stand the sight of myself. I think about the ways I've fallen short. The people I've let down. The people I've hurt. But when you find someone you can talk to...I don't know. Things seem less lonely. Just a little less...imperfect."

Monica was quiet for a moment, but she hadn't stopped stroking his chest. The feeling of her cool, smooth hands on him made him go half-staff almost without his realizing it.

"That's your problem right there, cowboy," she said at last.

"What?"

"You're chasing perfection," she said. "There's no such thing. Only imperfection. Beauty in imperfection, that's the best we can hope to find."

He took a deep breath and let it out slowly. "That and someone to talk to."

"And sex."

He smiled. "Damn fine sex."

She slapped his thigh gently. "You know, you didn't answer my question."

"The answer'ed scare you off, princess."

"I don't scare easily."

"Bullshit." He laughed. "You're scared of mud under your feet."

She looked up at him like he hung the moon right after he'd kicked her dog. He was fascinated by the way emotions played across her face like stage actors who weren't quite sure of their cues.

"But I'm not scared of you," she whispered.

"Don't I know it," he said, taking her in his arms again.

* * *

They stopped in Lake Isabella for tacos and Cokes. When they got back into the truck and started for Oleander, it was nearly six o'clock. Slapping Dean away as he kissed her neck and tried to distract her, Monica left a message for the sheriff asking him to hang on to the sign mock-ups until Monday.

"I'm not taking you home." Dean was sunburned, happy and randy as a rutting bull. "I'm checking us into a motel for the night."

"I'm staying with my parents," she said. "I can't just wander off for the night without there being retribution. Recriminations. Public shaming."

"You're thirty-two years old!"

"Yeah, thanks for reminding me," she said, laughing. "But I'm living at home now. Mommy's rules. *Papa ji*'s curfew."

They drove down the road a few minutes while Dean brainstormed ideas. "I've got it. Take out your phone. Call them and tell them this clown drank too much bourbon at Bo Walker's ranch and the old man's putting us up for the night—separate rooms, of course. His wife is there. She's making us a chicken potpie. It's really tasty. Can't say no. It'd be rude."

"You want me to lie to my parents?" she said, raising her eyebrow at him.

"*Lie* is a mighty strong word," he said. "I want you to protect their delicate sensibilities."

The business hotel in Bakersfield was newly remodeled, as sterile and clean as a blank sheet of paper. After a quick stop at the drugstore across the street, Dean checked them in, grabbed Monica out of the truck and kissed her the entire elevator ride up to the fourth floor.

"Ain't gonna be nothing left of you in the morning but that pretty face and a great, big satisfied smile," he whispered into her ear.

She kissed his neck. "I can't wait." She reached behind him and squeezed his ass hard as the elevator bell dinged.

As soon as the door of the hotel room clicked shut, they fell on each other, grabbing at each other's clothes. Dean sat on the bed and Monica pulled off his boots; he wrapped his arm around her waist and spun her onto the mattress, stripping off her jeans as she giggled. In a heartbeat, they were naked, panting and staring at each other like wolves.

"Come on," he said, picking her up and throwing her over his shoulder as she squealed. "Let's get this polliwog water off."

She contented herself with cussing him out and spanking his butt while he turned on the water in the shower. He put her in the bathtub and stepped in with her, pulling the curtain closed behind him. As steam filled the tiny room, he kept his eyes on hers as he poured shampoo into his hands. He lathered up her long black hair, working the white foam with his fingers and rinsing it all away. She rubbed the tiny bar of hotel soap between her palms and ran her hands all over his body, dragging her fingertips through his chest hair, over his abs and down over his hard-on. She gave him a few healthy pumps, and when he was as stiff as a baseball bat, she knelt down, reached between his legs and soaped up his balls.

"I hope you thank God every day for what you've got going on down here," she said. "This is the biggest dick I've ever seen." She reached behind him and slipped her soapy fingers up and down his ass crack.

He whooped softly. "You wicked little thing."

She rinsed him off, took hold of his cock with a sweet two-handed overhand grip and began to work him hard. As he looked down at her, she locked eyes with him and slipped the head of his cock into her pretty mouth. Her lips stretched into a tight O around him. When she began to suck him in rhythm with her strokes, he nearly slipped backwards and slammed his head into the tile wall.

He was no stranger to blowjobs. But this one was in a league all its own. Drunk with pleasure, Dean grabbed on to the showerhead for balance and held on.

She narrowed her eyes at him for a moment before closing them. Droplets of water stuck to her long dark eyelashes. As she slid her head down and up his shaft, she tightened her grip on the base of his cock and used her tongue to lash at the thick ridge on the underside of his dick. The rhythm was hypnotic, broken only by the fact that she was taking him deeper and deeper with each pull. She went down on him so long and so hard, motes began to swim in his eyes. When his dick knocked against the back of her throat, he took her wrists gently and pulled himself from her mouth.

"You can't expect me to hold back if you do things like that, princess." There was a tightness in his voice that he hadn't heard before.

Carefully, he helped her to her feet and kissed her. He wrapped his hands around her hair and pulled her head back slightly. The angle opened her up, and he probed her magical mouth with his tongue as she moaned and stroked his back.

The hot water had filled the bathroom with steam. Dean felt like he was wrapped up in a cloud of pure pleasure, like he had died and floated up to the version of heaven he'd always hoped for.

He reached down and stroked her slick breasts. Droplets clung to the tips of her nipples. When he saw this, Dean's balls tightened. He imagined coming all over those magnificent tits, his white come painting her skin in thick, hot drops.

With a sharp intake of breath, he reached behind her and turned off the water.

"Bedtime, princess," he said.

She wrapped her hair in a white towel and let him carry her back to the bed. Their clothes were scattered all over the hotel room. He had dropped the paper bag from the drugstore on the ground right by the door.

"What's in there?" she asked, raising herself up on her elbows.

He picked up the bag and, keeping his eyes on her, took out the contents one by one. He placed each item in a line on the chest of drawers.

A bottle of lube. Extra large.

A box of condoms, thirty-six count. Extra large.

Two bottles of Gatorade. Orange and lemon-lime. Extra large.

She laughed and held out her arms. "Come here."

They made out and goofed off until daylight faded to dark blue. Monica turned on the bedside lamp. Dean lay back, blinking at her as she stood up and removed the towel from her hair. She opened the box of condoms, pulled one out and picked up the bottle of lube. Grinning, she climbed back into bed with him. When he tried to go down on her, she wiggled away.

"Nope," she said, giving him a quick kiss on the mouth. "This is a two-way street, cowboy. It's my turn."

Her cheeks were rosy as she bent down and grabbed the base of his dick. His shaft grew and tightened in her pretty, dark hand; his cockhead swelled as she slid it into her mouth. He shut his eyes. Her damp hair fell heavy and cool over his stomach. She flicked her tongue against the tip of his cock and he jerked against the mattress.

When he started to throb, she removed him with a soft pop, straddled his legs and opened the condom. She rolled it on him, uncapped the bottle of lube and drizzled some on him like his dick was an ice-cream sundae.

"I like it this way," she said softly.

All he could manage was a grunt.

Gently, she rubbed the lube all over the rubber with her fingertips. She lifted herself up, grabbed his cock and worked him into her tight pussy, hissing softly between her teeth as her body strained to accommodate him. When he was halfway in, she moved her hips a little, front and back, stretching herself out as she shut her eyes tight and planted her hands flat against his chest for balance.

Dean stared, transfixed. The women who wandered into his bed usually made love like porn stars—all posing and vamping and cartoonish moaning and baby talk. They rarely if ever picked up on his cues about what actually turned him on. Most of them were so concerned with their own pleasure that he often felt used afterwards, as though the only reason they'd wanted to sleep with him was to brag to their friends they'd bagged a rodeo cowboy.

Well, sort of a cowboy—a rodeo clown. Close enough.

But Monica was different. Sweet and unguarded, she wanted to please him. She was passionate and hungry and even a little awkward. She wasn't concerned with her appearance in bed. Instead of worrying about how her hair or makeup looked, about how her body bent or twisted or curved, she gave herself completely to him and to their shared pleasure, totally unselfconscious and hornier than an alley cat in heat.

He reached up and combed her hair back with both his hands. She held on to his forearms and let her weight drag her down onto his cock as far as she could go. Together they shut their eyes and moaned at the onslaught of pleasure, at the deep penetration of his body into hers. Her pussy was gloriously tight. It took all of Dean's powers of control not to blow his load right then and there.

Her eyes fluttered open and latched on to his. Dean swiped his thumb slowly across her mouth, pressing the pad against her plum-colored lower lip. He dragged her lip down gently, exposing her pretty lower teeth.

"Open," he whispered.

The smooth, tight muscles of her pussy crushed his cock as he slid his thumb into her mouth. After she sucked it, staring him down with eyes as dark as coal, he plucked it from her lips, reached down and began to draw tiny circles on her hard little clit.

She whimpered, placed her hands on his thighs and leaned back, popping her hips forward slightly and showing him where his dick was buried deep between the rosy folds of her sex.

"Gorgeous," he murmured.

And then she began to ride him.

Tentatively at first, she undulated her hips. Mesmerized, he reached forward with his other thumb and softly pulled back the outer lips as he continued to stroke her clit. She squeezed him harder. Moisture from her arousal began to drip down onto his balls. She found her rhythm and began to ride him harder, the insides of her thighs slapping against his hips and her gorgeous tits and hard nipples bouncing madly above him.

"Jesus Christ," he hissed.

She threw her head back and ground her teeth. With each passing minute, she grew wetter and hotter around him. Soon they were both sweating. The room grew steamy with the heat of their fucking. Dean wouldn't be able to hold back much longer.

He sat up against the pillows, changing the angle so she could grind against the top of his cock and his pubic bone. Still rubbing her clit with his thumb, he dragged his middle finger through the pool of lube at the base of his dick and reached behind her.

"Can I touch you here?"

She looked down at him, eyes blazing. "You can do more than touch me there, if you want."

Gently, he stroked her tight opening until it flared at his touch. With firm, steady pressure, he pushed his middle finger into her up to the first joint. She bore down, both on his finger and his dick, and he threw his head back on the pillows and grunted, struggling not to come, even though the first tremors of a big orgasm tingled up and down his spine.

Monica pulled herself up off her knees and planted her feet flat on the mattress. She began to ride him hard, almost all the way up his shaft before slamming back down. The sound, the smell, the sensation of her lit up Dean's nervous system like the Fourth of July. Too turned on to see straight, he pushed his finger deeper in and quickened his thumb on her clit. She arched her back, hard. Her nipples shrank to tiny points. She shut her eyes and moaned deep and low in her chest.

"That's it," he whispered.

In a half second she was coming like a thrashing mountain lion, digging her nails into his thighs. The orgasm seized every muscle in her body, and she bucked against him like she was being electrocuted. God, she was beautiful when she came. He'd never get tired of watching it.

Trembling, she slid up and off him. Before she could collapse into a heap, he picked her up and placed her on all fours in the middle of the bed. As the last of her orgasm rippled through her, he buried his cock in her pussy, delighting in the resistance her body. He took the bottle of lube and squirted some directly into her, filling her ass with clear gel.

"Can I?" he said softly.

"Hell, yes," she murmured, fisting her hands into the sheets.

As he thrust into her slowly and deeply, he worked his thumb into her tiny opening.

"Ever been fucked here, princess?"

She shook her head. "No. Always curious about it, though."

A thrill passed through him as he thought about the nights he could spend training her. He wiggled his thumb gently and she squirmed beneath him. She was snug as hell.

"Not tonight," he said. "But if you want it, I'll show you. Soon." He reached forward with his free hand and swept her hair off her neck, exposing her back. He stroked her smooth skin and squeezed one of her ass cheeks. She squeezed him back—both his dick and his thumb.

"I'd like that, Dean," she said, her voice a hoarse whisper. "I want you. Every way. Every way you want to give it to me. I want it too."

Who is this woman?

Every one of his muscles was twitching from the effort of holding back. Slowly, Dean withdrew his thumb, reached down, grabbed her hips and took a deep breath.

"I'm going to come," he said softly.

"Do it."

He fucked her hard. After two-dozen strokes, his orgasm bucked out of its chute, tearing him up like a monster that was too wild to ride and too big to handle. He came in endless hot shots of come that shredded him from the inside out. When he finally collapsed onto the bed, Dean felt vulnerable and raw, trampled by lust.

In the darkness, Monica reached for him and held him tightly. The words came out before he knew what he was saying.

"I haven't been this happy in a long time."

He almost flinched when he heard himself. But the expression of naked emotion didn't scare her. Nothing seemed to scare her.

"I feel the same way," she whispered.

* * *

Homemade potato salad and fried chicken. The paper plate that Dean's mother handed to him drooped under the weight of a double portion of each.

"Looks good, Ma," he said, "but I can't eat all this."

Cecilia MacKinnon was wearing a sparkly red-and-blue T-shirt and a dazzling smile to match. Her long brown hair was coiled into a neat bun decorated with rhinestone stars. "In high school you would've come back for seconds."

"Must've had a tapeworm or something."

"Aw, hush. Don't be gross."

"Sorry. Thanks." He kissed the top of his mother's head before she turned to feed the rest of his brothers.

Dean looked around at the crowd gathered on the track at Oleander High School. Familiar faces, grown older. New kids he hadn't met before. Everyone was in attendance, from migrant workers in town for the season to families who'd farmed the Central Valley for generations. All had come out for a picnic and to watch the annual Fourth of July fireworks launch.

He sat down in a camp chair next to his father and started on his supper.

"Look at her," Dale MacKinnon said with a grin. "Your mom is a stunner, ain't she?"

Dean's parents had always been affectionate, so to hear his dad doling out sugar was nothing new. Dean took a bite and watched his mother handing out plates, surrounded by family. She looked happier than she had in months. Then he looked at his dad. The big bear of a man he'd grown up with looked thin and pale, worn down by chemotherapy and illness. But Dale's clothes were neatly pressed and his boots and belt buckle were polished to a high sheen. In his new white hat, he carried himself with the same pride he always displayed, in sickness or in health.

"So I heard you're part of the show tonight," Dale said.

"Yeah, but nothing special. Before the fireworks launch, the rodeo association's raffling off some prizes."

"What kind of prizes?"

"Passes to Oleander Rodeo Days and a meet-and-greet with Dandelion Wine at Walker Ranch. They want me to pick the tickets." He grinned. "I feel like I should be in an evening gown or something."

His dad snorted. "That'd cause a splash. Is Bo here tonight?"

"He'll be on stage with me."

"I'm surprised." Dale took a drink from a bottle of water. "Fourth of July is hard for him. Always has been."

Dean nodded. "Opening ceremonies at bull-riding shows—he's the same way. Too many pyrotechnics and stuff." He knew his old mentor had struggled with anxiety for years. According to Dean's father, Bo had come back from Vietnam a changed man. It was one of the

COWBOY RESURRECTION | 91

reasons he'd retired from bull riding and took up stock contracting instead.

"Dean!"

He looked up. Tottering her way through a minefield of picnic blankets and beer coolers, Monica headed straight for him. Her long black hair was loose and wild. She wore a modest but form-fitting navy-blue dress and sky-high red heels that made fireworks go off in funny places inside him.

Next to his mother, Dean's brother Clark raised his beer can toward Monica. "Hot damn. God bless America."

"Shut up, Clark," Dean said. He put down his plate and stumbled toward her like an idiot, but not before placing a small, well-placed kick to the underside of Clark's forearm. Beer splashed all over Clark's crotch.

"Oh, you fucker!" said Clark, hopping up.

"Watch your language!" their mother barked.

"Sorry, Ma." Clark corrected himself. "Oh, you gosh-darned fornicator."

Dean met Monica halfway and together they headed toward the event stage as she briefed him on what was going to happen. Using every excuse he could to touch her, he held her hand and put his other hand on the small of her back to steer her over the crowded field. With his thumb, he strummed the waistband of her panties through the fabric of her dress and fantasized about pulling her under the bleachers, yanking off her underwear and sinking himself balls-deep inside her.

She stopped talking. Maybe she asked him a question. She was looking at him like she expected an answer.

"Huh?" he asked.

She rolled her eyes at him. "I said, after I give my spiel, you turn the crank, open the little door and pull out the tickets. I'll announce the winners. After that, you and Bo sign autographs and take pictures until the fireworks start. The table is set up by the lemonade booth. Can you handle that?"

His hand crept a little lower and he gave her ass a tiny squeeze. "I think I can handle that, Miss Kaur."

A half-smile formed on her lips. "Behave yourself, please."

"Behave myself, huh?" He squeezed her again. "Let me ask you something. Did you wear this to embarrass me?"

She looked genuinely offended at that. "How is my outfit embarrassing?"

"No, princess. It's not the outfit." They finally made it backstage past the security guard. Performers and stage crew filled the small space, so Dean couldn't do what he wanted, but he did pull her close enough to whisper in her ear, "It's the giant hard-on you're giving me because you look so damn fine in it."

She said nothing, but a slight tremor ran through her, an aftershock to all the soul-shaking secret sex they'd had in the last three months.

Up on stage, the high school marching band finished up its spirited performance of Miley Cyrus's "Party in the USA". Dean leaned closer. "When can I see you again?"

Her breathing quickened. "Wait for my text."

"Bakersfield? Same place?"

She nodded and squeezed his hand. Dean remembered the feeling of both her hands in his as he pinned them up above her head. Tangled up in crisp motel sheets, they kissed as he drove into her like a madman. The old air conditioner struggled to keep up with them, the room sweltering with the heat of their fucking.

"I know what you're thinking," she whispered. "Down, boy. You'll be on stage soon."

He let go of her hand, took a step back and blew out a frustrated breath. "Yeah. You're right." He adjusted himself in his jeans. "Shit."

"Calm yourself," she said. "I'm going to go get Bo, okay?"

"Okay."

The raffle went exactly as Monica had planned. It had been a shrewd promotional stunt for the rodeo—the eyes of the entire community were on them, and all the proceeds from the raffle went straight to the high school music program. Dean sheepishly admitted to himself that it felt nice to be in front of a crowd again. Maybe he was a closet attention whore. He hoped not.

To his surprise, a long line of fans waited at the table for autographs when he and Bo sat down. Monica stood quietly behind them, his little mastermind, eyes on everyone and everything.

Somewhere around his fifth autograph, some kids waiting in line began to throw handfuls of poppers onto the asphalt. The explosion startled Bo, who dropped his marker on the ground. When Bo stooped to pick it up, Dean saw that his old mentor's hands had begun to shake.

"You okay?" Dean said quietly.

Bo looked up at him, an unfamiliar angry expression on his face. Anxiety ghosted his eyes. "I'm fine. I'm fine," he grumbled.

The fireworks display was going to be a big one—hundreds of explosions, the biggest in Oleander's history. Monica and Dean exchanged a look. She nodded at him, a slight nod filled with subtext, and Dean realized she was about to take control of the situation yet again.

Without hesitation, she stumbled forward slightly and caught herself by placing her hand on Bo's shoulder.

"Oh, God," she murmured. She closed her eyes and rubbed her temple with her thumb.

"Whoa, there," Dean said, playing along. He stood up at once and offered her his chair. She sat down.

"What's going on?" Bo said. He still looked agitated, but his tone softened when he saw that something was wrong with Monica.

She took a deep breath and let it out. "I just got really lightheaded there for a moment."

"Did you have anything to eat today?" Dean asked.

She nodded. "Breakfast. But...I'm on this new medication. Plus the heat and the crowd. I think everything is just getting to me."

Bo opened a bottle of water and handed it to her. "Drink this, honey."

She drank and made a face. "I hate to say it, but I don't think I can stay for the rest of the event."

"Dean, take her home," Bo said. "She's not well."

"No," she said. "Dean has to make sure we get all the information we need from the raffle winners and then he has to deliver the ticket money to Mrs. Martinez at the school. Could you take me home, Bo? I don't live far from here."

Chivalry trumped anxiety, and Bo stood up at once. "All right. Let's go. Take that water with you."

A grateful look on her face, Monica threaded her arm through Bo's and let him lead her out towards the parking lot. They were gone only minutes before the first rocket went off, a huge explosion of red-and-gold sparkles that lit up half the sky.

Dean greeted the last of his fans and took care of the odds and ends that Monica had assigned him. When he was finished, the fireworks show had already ended in a dazzling cascade of glitter and fire. Most families were packing up and ambling home. A few stragglers danced drunkenly on the grass, red cups in hand, while the grounds crew tried to shoo them away.

Dean walked up the empty bleachers and took a seat.

Years ago, he'd found an empty prescription bottle in Bo's truck. Lorazepam. Dean had looked it up. Doctors commonly prescribed the medication to veterans who suffered from PTSD. Dean had struggled with this knowledge. It took him a long time to understand that his tough-as-nails friend and mentor carried heavy burdens in private—deep wounds, decades old.

But Monica, as smart as she was, had understood at once. And even more than that, she knew how to protect Bo without damaging his pride.

Dean took off his hat, leaned back and looked up at a night sky still filled with the smoke and haze of spent fireworks. He took a deep breath and let it out slowly.

He'd never met anyone like her. She was amazing.

And just his luck that both of them were stuck here only in passing, two roads intersecting in the middle of nowhere on their way to somewhere else.

He took his phone out of his pocket and tapped out a text. *You're slick as hell.*

Her response came back a few seconds later. *I know.*

Dean stared at the screen, trying to think of a funny rejoinder. He couldn't. Something warm and heavy had lodged in his chest, something deeper than affection, something stronger than respect. Something he hadn't allowed himself to feel in a long, long time.

Thank you, princess.

He smiled at her reply. *You're welcome, cowboy.*

CHAPTER THREE

Wildflowers

*If dreams were lightning and thunder was desire, this old
house would have burnt down a long time ago...*

—JOHN PRINE

Dean stood at the foot of the bed with his arms
folded. "How're you doing?"

She smiled. "Never better."

He'd bound Monica's arms behind her back with
rope. Completely naked, she sat on the mattress propped
up against a pile of pillows, legs spread wide open.

They were in Bakersfield for another nooner. So far,
they'd made love back at the river and deep in the woods,
in the hot springs off the Kern River south of Lake
Isabella, in his family's old pole barn, in his childhood

bedroom while the rest of the family was at church, in his brother's truck, in his father's truck, in the back seat of her Prius, even behind the Silver Spur one drunken night when they were both feeling brave. But the hotel was home base—the place they came to play hard.

Dean found Monica's body endlessly fascinating. He loved her soft, graceful curves, her brown skin and wild black hair, her dark nipples and the silken hair that grew at her sex. He suspected that he was becoming addicted to her pussy, if that were possible—he could spend hours touching her, stroking her, looking at her, tasting her.

He knelt down, spread her open with his fingertips and stared at her with what he suspected was a mooncalf expression on his face.

"You act like you've never seen one," she said.

"Not like yours."

It was true. Her pussy reminded him of a sweet plum with a shiny, cherry-pink center.

She tried to wiggle out of his knots—no luck. Vulnerable and earthy, she was the woman of his wickedest dreams, all trussed up and ready to play.

"What do you want, princess?" he asked, undoing his belt buckle.

"You, cowboy."

He undressed in a hurry and climbed into bed with her. He covered her neck with kisses and feasted on her beautiful breasts, leaving her nipples erect and wet, loving her up until she was squirming. The ropes creaked as she pulled on her bindings.

"You tryin' to get away from me?" he asked, kissing her throat.

"No. I want to touch you."

"Too bad."

He reached down and began to stroke her delicate clit. Soaking wet, her tight pussy gave way to one finger, then another. He bent his fingers slightly and massaged her G-spot. The ropes went taut as she curled into herself. Her sex began to throb, the pulses of her body speeding toward release.

God, he loved to make her come like this, giving it to her as hard as she gave it to him. After weeks of endless, ecstatic practice, he could make her body do all kinds of things.

But today, he was trying something new.

Gently, he withdrew his fingers and picked up the toy on the nightstand.

"Where'd you get this?" he asked.

"San Francisco."

"Why'd you choose this one?"

She opened her eyes and looked at him as he switched her vibrator on and off. It was expensive, a sleek pink silicone job with four speeds. "It was quiet," she said.

He nodded. "Quiet toy, loud woman." He put the vibrator down on the bed and picked up the bottle on the nightstand. With a generous hand, he doused her with lube. He could sense her excitement as he spread himself with more lube before capping the bottle and putting it back on the nightstand.

"Tell me if—"

"Yes, I know. I'll tell you if it hurts," she said impatiently, twisting in her bindings.

He cocked an eyebrow at her as he began to jack himself off with languid strokes. "You in a hurry to be somewhere?"

She stared at his cock in his hand. "I'm in a hurry to feel you inside me."

Her hunger mirrored his. She captivated him with her sensuality, her eagerness to explore. She was nowhere near as sexually experienced as he was, but she was eager to close the gap, and fast. He slipped on a condom and picked up the toy.

On its lowest setting, the vibrator purred softly as he ran it over the tender, flared lips of her pussy. Slowly, he slid it into her, thrusting in rhythm to the pumps of his hand around his shaft. She whimpered and shut her eyes tight. Dean kept his eyes open, thrilled by the sight of her sex wrapped hungrily around the smooth pink toy.

With a soft pop, he pulled it from her and pressed its tip to her clit. Monica gasped and arched her back.

"Open your eyes," he said, and she did.

With his free hand, he guided the head of his cock into her tiny ass. As soon as her tight ring of muscle gave way, he slid his hips forward and thrust into her inch by slow inch until he was buried inside her as far as he could go. He pulled out halfway, then gave her a quick, brutal thrust, tapping her with a wet smack. She shut her eyes again and groaned.

"You okay?" he whispered.

She nodded. "I'm okay."

He was breathing like he'd run a race. He thrust again. Then once more. Goose bumps rose on her skin and her nipples grew harder. Insane with lust, he turned up the setting on her vibrator and slid it back into her pussy. Her snug ass clenched wetly around him. The feeling drove him out of his mind. He adjusted the angle of the slick little vibrator until its shaft rubbed against her clit. When she threw her head back and began to breathe between her teeth, he started to fuck her hard, stretching her to her limits and pushing himself to his.

"I'll never get enough of this," he snarled. He shoved the vibrator in and out of her like a piston. Sweat blurred his vision. His blood had turned to fire. "I'll never get enough of you."

"Oh, God," she whispered, "Dean, I'm gonna come."

He looked at her as she balanced on the precipice, lips parted, eyes glazed. So beautiful and alive. His Monica.

At once, all of her inner muscles began to convulse, squeezing him so hard he thought he'd pass out from the pleasure of it. When he looked into her eyes, he lost control. His own orgasm jetted out, hot and wild. With his free hand, he gripped the edge of the mattress and fucked her without holding back, riding out his climax to its last shuddering drop.

Spent, he collapsed on top of her, still inside her. The toy slid out of his grasp and rolled onto the sheets. When he finally caught his breath, she kicked him lightly with her heel.

"Come on, big boy," she whispered. "Untie me before you fall asleep."

He opened his eyes and blinked at her. "What? Huh? You'll be all right. Just hang tight there."

"Dean!" she barked, trying to wiggle away.

"So...tired...g'night, princess." He feigned sleep and rested his full weight on her as she squealed with laughter.

* * * * *

After a quick shower together, they climbed back into bed for a few more minutes of peace before they had to get dressed and return to work. Monica pressed her back against Dean's warm chest as he spooned her, his heavy arms wrapped tightly around her and his beard tickling the back of her neck as he spoke.

"Bo told me to thank you for arranging all those interviews," he said, stroking her stomach with the back of his thumb. "He says it's been nonstop reporters since you made those calls."

"His bulls attract good press," she murmured. "I can't believe it all starts next week. I feel like we've been planning this rodeo forever."

"You did a good job, princess. You did everything right. I'm impressed—the whole town is."

She snorted softly. "You've done half of it. And there's still a million things that could go wrong, so...withhold your awe."

He kissed her shoulder and tightened his hold on her. "Withhold my awe for you? Nope. Never."

"You and that cowboy sugar." Monica closed her eyes as he slid his thigh between hers. As soon as they'd started sleeping together, a heavy knot of pain had lodged itself in her chest. The deep ache had only intensified as the days passed, speeding toward their inevitable goodbye and her upcoming move back to Silicon Valley. They hadn't talked about it, but both she and Dean knew their particular lease on happiness was almost up.

The pain was bittersweet in light of the secret truth that Monica had forced herself to face.

She'd fallen in love with Dean MacKinnon.

It was hopeless. She loved every damn thing about him. Those eyes as blue as a high desert sky; the strength and grace of his body; his bottomless, shameless lust. But she loved his quietness too. His steady, watchful presence calmed her.

It made sense—his job was to protect others from danger like some kind of cowboy guardian angel. Dozens of bull riders whose lives he'd saved in the arena would attest to that.

But what Monica loved most about him was a quality she couldn't quite define. There was a sweet kind of sadness about him, as though he believed his story was already over but he was perfectly content being a minor character in the stories of other people. Dean never wanted to be the center of attention. He had no idea that this humility made him even more mythic, more heroic to his fans—and even more attractive to her.

Who wouldn't fall in love with a man like him?

Monica bit back the flash of pain she felt whenever she thought about all the women who must have walked on this road before her. She'd be gone, soon too. Just another short chapter in his life, over and done.

"What's the matter?" he asked softly.

"Nothing," she lied. "A little hungry is all."

He reached over her and checked his cell phone. "We've got an hour before the meeting with the security company. You want to grab a bite with me?" He gave her a kiss on the forehead.

"Sounds good," she said.

* * *

Dean put his clothes on and sat in the corner of the hotel room to watch Monica as she got dressed. She wiggled into her underwear, then pulled on a light-blue blouse with tiny pearl buttons. She slid on her black skirt and stepped into her fancy snakeskin high heels.

"Do you have anything to wear to the rodeo?" he asked.

"I was planning on picking something up at the Western-wear store before we left Bakersfield. Maybe after the meeting."

"You'd make one sexy cowgirl."

She paused. "Should I make the inappropriate joke or should you?"

"What joke is that?"

"You're the cowboy, I'm the Indian."

He groaned and threw a pillow at her. After putting on her earrings, she brushed her hair, braided it and applied some lip gloss, puckering her lips goofily in the mirror. Dean stared, his heart sputtering like an old engine and his head trying desperately to shut it back down.

Don't. Don't fucking say a thing. She's leaving next week.

It was getting harder and harder to hide the truth. He'd fallen for her. Not the way he'd fallen for his ex-wife, all adrenaline and goo-goo eyes, but a slow, all-consuming way, like an enormous bonfire burned down to its red-hot embers.

Monica was a grown woman—maybe that was most of it. She was smart and quick and funny and fearless. She didn't need him to prop her up or show her off when she was feeling down. Independent and tough, she could take care of herself. It made her sexy as hell.

Sex had always been an important theme in his life. In Monica, he had found a partner who shared his deep hunger, his need to play hard. She wasn't ashamed of his past. Sometimes, she even asked him about it—it turned her on. What was his first time like? What was his wildest night? Had he ever had a threesome? Had he ever been with a guy?

He always answered her honestly. At first, he was afraid to share his memories with her. But the more they talked about it, the more comfortable he became answering her questions. In a strange way, it was as if all his experiences had prepared him for *this* experience—for the experience of being with her.

Dean wanted to tell her the truth.

He loved her.

For days, the words had lived on his tongue like canaries trapped in the mouth of a cat.

Enjoy the last few days with her. Don't complicate things. Don't make this harder than it needs to be.

He put on his hat, cleared his throat and stood up. "Ready, princess?"

With a naughty smile, she slipped her sex toy and the silk rope into her enormous tote bag. Hand in hand, they left the hotel room. In the parking lot by his brother's truck, Dean wrapped his arms around her waist and yanked her close for one more wicked kiss. She wiggled her tongue against his. With a grunt, Dean grabbed her ass with both hands and squeezed hard as she giggled against his lips.

The screech of tires yanked Dean out of his trance. Without thinking, he grabbed Monica and swung her out of the path of the silver minivan coming right at them. The van stopped short, just inches from the truck.

Two tall men wearing beards and turbans got out of the car. The younger one had been driving. He pulled a Bo Duke and nearly slid across the hood, landing on his feet and putting a finger in Dean's chest.

"Get your hands off my sister," he said. He was a little paunchy and looked to be in his late twenties. He got right in Dean's face, and his dark eyes flashed with rage.

"Take it easy," said the older man. "Monica, get in the van."

Dean looked at Monica. Her eyes were wide and she'd gone pale as a bedsheet. "Papa—"

Holy shit. For a moment, Dean wished that he were in the arena facing down a furious bucking bull. At least he'd know what to do.

The older man's voice was deep and calm. "*Beti,* now."

To Dean's surprise, Monica's shoulders fell. "I'm sorry," she whispered to him. Then she turned and got into the minivan, a mortified expression on her face.

Dean turned to Monica's father. "Mr. Singh, your daughter and I, we've been seeing each other for a while." He swallowed hard. *Consensual* seemed like too inappropriate a word to use in this situation. "I assure you she's not here with me...against her will." Dean almost groaned as the words left his mouth. *Great. Like that's any better than* consensual, *you idiot.*

Though he wasn't aggressive like Monica's brother, Monica's father spoke with the kind of authority that Dean imagined made other men sit down and listen. "Mr. MacKinnon, this is a family matter. I appreciate your concern for my daughter, but you cannot see her again. It is not possible."

Dean was dumbstruck for a moment. Monica's brother took one step closer, crowding him.

"I don't mean any disrespect, Mr. Singh," Dean said slowly, "but your daughter is an adult. She's the one who should make that decision."

"My daughter understands what her obligations are. I'm sure this was a nice romance for her. But it ends now. She'll make that decision because she knows it's the right one." Without another word, Monica's father turned and got back into the van.

Monica's brother put his finger in Dean's chest once more. "Touch her again and see what happens, MacKinnon. My sister's not one of your skanks."

Dean turned his attention on Monica's brother for the first time. He leveled his gaze and lowered his voice. "Watch it."

"Ravinder! Let's go!" shouted Monica's father.

Monica's brother sneered. He turned back to the van, started it up and drove away, leaving Dean standing in the parking lot alone.

* * *

Monica's mother sat at the kitchen table, her eyes red and swollen. It was nearly midnight. Spread out before her were stacks of printouts, dating profiles organized according to geographical location, age and profession.

"You said your office was in Cupertino, so I searched Cupertino. I searched Sunnyvale, Mountain View, San

Jose, Santa Clara. I asked around. I made phone calls. You said you didn't want a doctor. What kind of woman doesn't want to marry a doctor? I said, fine. So I found engineers. Attorneys. College professors. For you! All for you!" Fresh tears began to stream down her mother's face. "Why? Why do you punish us this way? What haven't we done for you? What haven't we given you?"

After putting all their kids to bed, Ravinder and his wife Harpal had come to sit at the kitchen island with the sole purpose of looking accusingly at Monica. Her father leaned against the kitchen counter, his arms folded, his features stony and hard to read.

"You've already missed one chance at getting married. You're thirty-two years old! Time is running out!" her mother screeched. "Why are you so intent on ruining your life?"

"Calm down," said Monica's father. "You're going to wake up the little ones."

Monica stared at all the profiles on the table, Sikh men in turbans and beards, some clean-shaven, some young, some old, some handsome, some homely. Her mother saw this as her future—her only path.

"What I want to know is, why Dean MacKinnon?" Ravinder said. "He's disgusting. You probably caught VD."

"Don't disrespect your sister." Monica's father sat down at the table next to her and rubbed his beard. "It's getting late. This is the situation as it stands. You will move to Cupertino next week, as you have been planning to do. Until then, as you complete the preparations for the rodeo, Ravinder or Harpal will drive you around town and accompany you on your business."

Monica leaned forward. "A chaperone? Papa, this is not right—"

"What is not right is that I had to hear from our neighbor's grandmother's hairdresser that her sister saw you checking into a hotel in the middle of the day. The hotel where you have been carrying on, doing who knows what with that—that cowboy!" Monica's mother howled and wiped her eyes with a moist ball of Kleenex. "*Tenu sharam nahi aundi?* Don't you have any shame? You think that what you do doesn't have repercussions. It does. A scandal like this? People talk. Let's just hope you can outrun the scandal before it reaches the Bay Area."

Monica kept her eyes on the tabletop, silently hoping this so-called scandal would circle the globe twice before she had to meet any of the men her mother had chosen for her.

"Please understand where we're coming from," said Monica's father. He took her hand and gave it a gentle squeeze. "What you are doing is not right, *beti*. This is not the way to love, sneaking around like thieves. You need to end things now. It will be better for both of you in the long run."

That night, as she lay sleepless in her bed, Monica put the covers over her head and turned on her phone. Four texts and a voicemail from Dean. She read the texts first.

Are you all right? What can I do?

Should I come over and talk to your dad?

Call me when you can.

I'll be up late. Call or text anytime.

The voicemail was short, just her laconic cowboy speaking quietly, as though he were in a place where a lot of people could hear him. A TV was on in the background, and the voices of kids talking quietly to adults.

"Hi. It's me. Just, ah, hoping everything's all right. You looked pretty upset this afternoon. Call me. Okay. Bye."

Just then her phone buzzed. Another text.

I miss you.

Her bedroom was right next to her nieces' room. She couldn't call Dean without waking them up. Her fingers flew as she composed a message for him.

I can't talk, but don't worry. I'm fine. My family's pretty furious at me. Nothing new.

She paused, not sure how to proceed.

I'll be around, but it'll be hard for us to see each other alone.

An understatement. She'd be lucky if her brother or her sister-in-law would let her go to the bathroom by herself.

I'm so sorry about everything. This isn't how I wanted things to turn out.

Gossiping neighbors had cheated her and Dean out of their last few days together, but they both knew their time was coming to an end. Was her father right? Should she say goodbye now? She ached so hard she could barely breathe.

But maybe it'd better if we

Tears formed in her eyes but she fought back the urge to sob. Dean would try to fix things. But how could he? This was an impossible situation. She had to protect him. She finished the sentence.

But maybe it'd better if we ended things now.

It'd be cleaner this way, she decided. No more sneaking around. No more pretending they could be a couple when they couldn't. She pressed *send* before she lost her nerve but not before her heart crumbled to powder in her chest.

His reply came back almost instantaneously.

Is this what you want?

No. She wanted *him*. She wanted to walk down the street holding his hand for everyone to see. She wanted to sleep next to him at night and wake up in the morning looking into his eyes. She wanted to spend long afternoons bullshitting and laughing and making love with him. She wanted to talk about the future with him as though it were something they could share.

But his life was here, and his home was on the road. He didn't belong in the city any more than she belonged out in the middle of a rodeo arena.

Six years she'd worked to get this job in Cupertino. Building relationships. Wheeling and dealing. Impressing every single person she'd ever come into contact with in the industry. And the company wanted her enough that they'd waited for her.

There was no point in pretending she and Dean could be together. They couldn't.

This is what I want, she texted back.

One minute passed, then two. Her pillow was wet with tears. Her phone buzzed once more.

See you at the rodeo.

* * *

Trailers, trucks and pens filled the enormous lot next to the rodeo arena. A summer rainstorm had soaked the grounds and slick, caramel-colored mud covered absolutely everything, but no one seemed to mind. As long as the arena was in good condition, the show would go on.

Monica's sister-in-law, Harpal, was about as exciting as sitting on a curb and staring at a stop sign. Like a dutiful little trooper, she followed closely as Monica criss-crossed the grounds to make sure everything went as smoothly as possible. Harpal, in her chinos and flats, was soaked and miserable. Monica, in a hat, jeans and new cowboy boots from Bakersfield, felt right at home in the mud.

As Monica made her rounds, some of the visiting competitors, all fit young cowboys, flirted openly with her. They invited her for drinks at the Silver Spur or at their trailers after the next round. Flattered, she turned them down under Harpal's indignant gaze.

"They're so dirty," her sister-in-law said under her breath. "Disgusting."

Monica wholeheartedly disagreed with her, but none of the handsome cowboys came close to the only one she was looking for in the crowd.

Because of Monica's careful planning and orchestration, the opening parade and all the events went according to plan. Bo Walker's bulls were crowd-pleasers, and the commentators and barrel man kept the huge crowd's attention.

All around her, Monica heard the *ka-ching* of ringing registers—concessions, alcohol, merchandising, tickets, entry fees, sponsorships. She smiled as she thought about all that money flowing into Oleander. The Rambling Ranch Inn was fully booked. Looking into the stands, she was proud to see, scattered here and there among the cowboy hats, a few Sikhs in turbans, enjoying their day at the rodeo with their families.

She was on her way to the VIP box when she finally saw the person she was searching for.

Dean stood by the chutes. He was chatting with Bo Walker and the young bullfighters hired by Miller-Davis for the bull-riding events. A crowd of bronc riders and bull riders had gathered around him too. They hung on every word he said. Women and kids in the stands leaned over to ask Dean for autographs and photos. He had a friendly smile for every single person who approached him.

Monica wasn't prepared for the pain that flooded her from head to toe when she saw Dean. He was so handsome that looking at him sharpened her senses. He was wearing a white straw hat, a freshly pressed blue shirt and one of his championship belt buckles. Even from afar, his dark beard couldn't hide the sharp lines of his cheekbones or the strong angle of his jaw.

The commentators spotted him from the announcing stand. One of the event's cameramen rushed over to get a shot for the big screen.

"And here today is Oleander's very own Dean MacKinnon, two-time freestyle bullfighting world champion. Looks like he's giving our Miller-Davis bull-fighters some pointers, there. Boys, listen up. You're getting schooled by the best. Ladies and gentlemen, let's give Dean a warm hometown welcome."

The crowd cheered. Dean waved at the camera and smiled. Monica heard some wolf whistles and ladylike shrieks from the audience.

When the camera cut away, Dean looked up and locked eyes with her. His smile faltered for a moment before he put it back on and turned back to Bo.

Almost gleefully, Harpal poked Monica in the ribs. "Come on. Stop looking at him. We're blocking traffic here on the stairway."

Monica frowned at her sister-in-law before turning and walking up the stairs.

* * *

Packed with people, the Oleander Community Center was sweltering. All the doors had been thrown open to let in fresh air. Visitors were stacked five deep for beer and whiskey at the bar. The band, Mason Crow and the Wildflowers, played nonstop boot-scootin' country, whipping the crowd into an energetic frenzy. Around the room, old-timers sat at tables, watching the younger people flirt and pair up on the dance floor.

After Harpal went home to put her kids to bed, Monica took a moment to sit with her father and uncles at a table near the door. Her Uncle Dev's truck wash and repair shop was a rodeo sponsor, as was the Rambling Ranch Inn. Though they didn't drink alcohol, her father and his brothers were having a good time. They congratulated her on all her hard work and enjoyed themselves making outrageous suggestions for next year's rodeo.

Laughing at her Uncle Dev's idea for "Turban Cowboy" T-shirts, she didn't notice the man standing behind her until her father said something.

"Mr. MacKinnon."

Monica stopped laughing, bolted upright in her chair and turned around. Dean touched the brim of his hat as he acknowledged each man at the table.

"Gentlemen," he said. "Mr. Singh. Nice to see you again. I was wondering if I might ask your permission to dance with your daughter."

Monica was speechless. After what had happened in the parking lot, Dean had enormous balls to approach her father and his six scowling brothers.

A long, uncomfortable moment of silence passed before Monica's father leaned forward and asked her, "*Beti*, do you want to dance with this boy?"

Dean wasn't a boy. And it had been decades since she'd been a girl. But Monica said, "Yes, Papa."

Her father looked at him, then at her. "One song. And then you must tell him goodbye."

"Sir." Dean nodded to her father and held out his hand. Monica took it. The crowd stared hotly as he led her onto the dance floor.

The band started a new song. Willie Nelson's "Crazy".

Dean put his hand on her waist and pulled her close. "Appropriate," he said softly.

She nodded, too sad to smile.

He led her in a graceful two-step. Their bodies melded together on instinct. They shared one rhythm and the sweet lilt of the music made Monica lightheaded in his arms.

"You look real pretty," he said. "I knew the cowgirl look would suit you."

Instead of speaking, she rested her cheek against his shoulder and concentrated on not falling to pieces in front of all these people.

"I'm so proud of you," he said. "What you've done here—it's amazing. The town needed this. The people needed this."

She didn't want to talk about the rodeo, so she squeezed his hand and said, "You're a good dancer."

"Most cowboys are." He added with a grin, "Good two-steppers, anyway."

Usually, she didn't care for country music. But in the last couple of months, Monica had changed in more ways than one. "I like this song."

"Me too."

They took another turn around the dance floor. With each note, their time together dwindled away. "I don't know how to say goodbye to you," she said, looking up into his eyes. "I don't think I can."

"Tell you what, then. Let's not say goodbye. The song will end. I'll go my way, and you'll go yours. And maybe no matter where we go, no matter where we end up, there will always be some part of us still here on this dance floor. Stuck in time. Dancing to 'Crazy'. How does that sound?"

Her laconic cowboy could be a poetic soul sometimes. One tear fell down her cheek. Dean caught it with his thumb and wiped it away.

His voice grew softer, just loud enough for her to hear. "That dream job. It's waiting for you. You've worked hard for it. You deserve it." He smiled. "I can't wait to see what you accomplish."

"I'm going to miss you so much," she said. The song slowed towards its inevitable end.

He kissed her lips. "I'm gonna to miss you too, princess."

As the band played the final chords of the song, the crowd began to applaud. When Monica opened her eyes, Dean let her go. His eyes on hers, he touched the brim of his cowboy hat and nodded. Without saying goodbye, he turned around and slid back into the crowd.

* * *

Two days later, Dean drove his father's old truck out of town, past the airfield east of the highway. On the outskirts of Oleander, the road he took cut through acres and acres of grapes. For generations, the Singhs had grown table grapes, green Thompson and red Flame and Summer Royal grapes so purple they were almost black. Monica's father had six brothers, all involved in the cultivation, processing or distribution of their family's grapes. Theirs was a tight, shrewd operation, the envy of farmers all over the Central Valley.

As Dean drew closer to Monica's family's house, he took control of his breath. He always did the same thing before a big show, right after he put on all his protective gear but before he got into the arena. Thirty deep, slow breaths, in and out. He cranked down the window and let in an early-evening breeze.

Breathe in, breathe out. One. Breathe in, breathe out. Two.

The exercise got blood flowing into his brain. But it also got his mind off any anxieties that would take him out of the game. He'd gotten into the habit a long time ago. His fellow bullfighters teased him about it, asking how far apart his contractions were so that they'd know when to pass out the cigars.

Set on the edge of a field facing the foothills, the Singh house was gleaming white, a large stucco house with an expensive-looking clay tiled roof. Its lush, green lawn contrasted with the dry earth surrounding it. A familiar silver minivan, a relatively new Mercedes Benz and a brand-new red F-150 were parked in the driveway. As Dean parked his truck in the turnaround, he took a mental note.

Appearances are important to the Singhs. Water and trim the lawn. Keep the cars clean.

He got out of his truck and took a quick look at his own appearance. He'd showered and ironed his clothes, but he hadn't cleaned his boots.

Shit. He shook his head and stuck his keys in his pocket. *Too late now.*

He walked up the slate steps to the double doors with brass handles. He took his thirtieth breath and blew it out slowly. Then he rang the doorbell.

A surly young woman he recognized as Monica's sister-in-law opened the door and eyed him suspiciously. "Yes. Can I help you?"

"Good evening, miss," he said. "I'm here to speak with Jasmohan Singh. He's expecting me."

The look she gave him should've come with a number to the poison control center. But she opened the door and said with a frown, "Come in."

He took off his hat and followed her into an empty living room.

"Sit down," said the young woman. "I'll get him."

The leather sofa sighed under Dean's weight. He looked around while he waited. The house was pristine. Thick Persian carpets covered polished marble tile. A mantel clock ticked loudly over the fireplace. He could see a faint reflection of himself in the plasma TV. He looked nervous. He put his hat on the seat next to him and tried to relax his shoulders a bit. As he was trying to figure out what to do with his hands, Monica's father walked in.

Dean stood up. "Mr. Singh."

The older man was wearing pressed slacks, a black polo shirt and topsiders. He wore a navy blue turban. He was handsome and imposing, a quintessential business-man and not the kind of salty rancher that Dean was used to dealing with around these parts. Reading glasses were perched at the end of his nose, perfect for peering over and looking disapprovingly at Dean, which he did as they shook hands.

"Mr. MacKinnon. Please, have a seat."

The two men sat down opposite one another. Monica's father sat on an armchair that held him at a slightly higher level. Dean understood the significance of this.

"I know why you're here," said the older man. "And while I respect your decency in coming to speak with me, I don't want to waste your time. You may not date my daughter. It's impossible."

Dean was expecting that. "May I ask your reasons?"

He raised his eyebrows. "Well, there's the obvious one. She's not here. She's moved back to Northern California, as you're well aware."

"Family obligations are keeping me here at the moment," Dean said. "But I would travel anywhere to be with her, if she would have me. And if I had your blessing."

"Which brings me to reason number two. I can't give you my blessing."

"You know my family. Is that the issue?"

"I know your mother and father. Good people. I know you too. Hard worker. Respected in your sport. Of course I admire that."

"But still not good enough for Monica?"

Monica's father leaned forward in his chair. "Please don't take offense at this, Mr. MacKinnon. My family settled in California almost a hundred years ago. The way we have kept our religion and our culture alive is by marrying people of the same background. This is how we continue, how we stay whole. If we hadn't maintained this tradition, our sense of identity, the very core of who we are would've been diluted, even lost. Do you understand?"

Here was where things got tricky. A few conversations with Monica and a couple of hours on Google formed the extent of Dean's knowledge of Sikhism. He didn't want to come across as a loudmouthed white boy. But he definitely didn't want to come across as a pushover. "Mr. Singh, Monica once told me that the word Sikh means student. Is this correct?"

He could see the old man's invisible hackles rising. "Yes. It does."

"She told me it's a religion of students, dedicated to learning the teachings of the gurus and studying the Sri Guru Granth Sahib."

"Mr. MacKinnon—"

"And I've read Sikhism teaches that people from all races are equal in the eyes of God."

"Equal, yes, but free to sleep with my daughter? No. That is not part of our religion." He leaned back in his chair and looked at Dean, his eyes clouded with contempt and pity.

"You have a point there." Dean looked up at the scowling man. He couldn't fault Mr. Singh for being angry. If he had a daughter as beautiful and brilliant as Monica, no man would ever be good enough for her. "To be honest, I'm surprised you and your brothers haven't beaten me to death with grape stakes and buried me in one of your vineyards."

Monica's father's features relaxed slightly. "The night's still young, Dean. I saw *Casino* too, you know. De Niro and Pesci. Good movie."

"Well, at least we agree on that." Dean took another deep breath, clearing the cobwebs out of his brain and putting him back on target. "I know you're a busy man, Mr. Singh, so I'll just get to the point. I'm not here to ask permission to see your daughter."

That got his attention. "You're not?"

"No. I'm here to ask permission to see you."

The older man sat up in his chair. "What?"

"Please, hear me out. I want to learn about you. You and your family. What you value. Who you are." He cleared his throat. "Monica loves you. She was so afraid of letting you down that she kept our relationship a secret, something she was ashamed of." He paused. "Mr. Singh, I don't want to be the kind of man she's ashamed of. I want to be the kind of man she would be proud to be seen with. And for that, I need to ask your help."

Jasmohan Singh narrowed his eyes, and Dean realized at once where Monica had gotten the shrewd sparkle in hers.

"What do you have in mind?" the older man asked.

* * *

September in Northern California. Monica missed the sun.

Her corner office had floor-to-ceiling windows, but there wasn't a lot to see besides traffic on De Anza Boulevard, the gas station across the street and overcast skies.

Her dream job wasn't what she had expected. A massive paycheck was nice, but there were underlying issues in the office. The cofounders of the startup weren't getting along. The office manager had disclosed to her that they were having trouble securing their third round of funding. The stress was starting to show.

She'd just completed her 10:30 conference call and was clicking through the quagmire in her inbox when a call came through from reception.

She picked it up. "Monica Kaur."

"Monica, you have a visitor." Shirley the receptionist sounded unusually giggly. "He says his name is...I'm sorry, what was your name again?" More giggles. "Dean MacKinnon."

Monica almost dropped her phone. She kicked her chair away from her desk and stood up, automatically fussing with her hair. "I...um..."

"Are you there?" Shirley asked.

"Yes, I'm here." Monica's brain raced. "Could you...maybe...could you walk him back to my office?"

"Yeah, sure."

Oh jeez. What is he doing here? Frantic, Monica dug in her purse for a compact. She dabbed powder over the bridge of her nose and tucked a few wild tendrils of hair back into her bun. Cursing, she slipped her shoes back on and swept the remains of her yogurt parfait into the trashcan.

She had just finished checking her teeth for stray raspberry seeds when the receptionist appeared at her office door.

"Here she is," Shirley said, all smiles.

Outside, heads popped up over cubicle walls like gophers in holes. Monica could hear her coworkers' curious whispers and stifled laughter. She stood up, and Shirley, still mooning, sidled quietly away.

The man who stood in the doorway was breathtaking. She'd daydreamed about him for two months, but the Dean she remembered was nothing compared to the reality of him.

For a moment, he stood statue still, staring at her with his bright blue eyes. Tall and jacked, he was wearing an ivory wool hat, a dark-blue shirt and crisp, dark jeans. He'd put on one of his championship buckles. A gray sports coat strained across his massive shoulders. He wore his usual shitkickers, but he'd cleaned and polished them.

In his arms, he carried a huge bouquet of wilting orange poppies wrapped in brown paper. A few delicate petals covered him like confetti.

As he leaned forward and kissed her cheek, she breathed him in. Her nervous system lit up like twinkle lights. He smelled like leather, old bay aftershave and sex, sex, sex.

"Hey," he said.

"I can't believe you're here." Her voice faltered.

"Yeah." He smiled. "Me neither."

Out of the corner of her eye, Monica spotted her officemates eavesdropping on them. She reached behind him, closed the door and lowered the shade that covered the glass wall. Knees trembling under her skirt, she walked back to her desk chair and pointed at the armchair by the window.

"Have a seat," she said, as though he were just another client instead of the man who'd been haunting her fantasies for eight weeks straight.

Before he sat down, he put the bouquet in her arms. "Um, for you." The petals rained down on her slate-colored carpet. For a moment she remembered the sun-scorched field covered with wildflowers and what it was like to see Dean shirtless for the first time. Her toes curled.

She put the flowers down on top of her stacks of file folders and reports. Their bright orange hue was intense. Suddenly, she realized that everything in her office, including the clothes she wore, were shades of gray. She'd been living without color since she'd left Oleander behind—since she'd left him.

"Why didn't you call to tell me you were coming?" she asked, even though she suspected she already knew the answer to that question.

"Didn't want to take the risk that you'd turn me away." He looked around the room. "Nice digs." When his gaze came to rest on her, his eyes narrowed slightly. "You look good, Monica."

Pleasure rippled through her, but she forced herself not to smile. "What are you doing here?"

He took off his hat and balanced it on his thigh. "I'm here because I need to talk to you. In person." He ran a hand through his thick, dark hair and cleared a frog out of his throat. He was nervous. Dean MacKinnon was never nervous. Monica had to admit it was a glorious thing to see.

"Here I am," she said, making her voice as placid as possible. "What's going on?"

"Okay. Remember that stuff I said during the dance, about you going your way and me going mine?"

"Yeah."

"Total bullshit." He rubbed the wool brim of his hat between his thumb and forefinger as he stared at her. "The truth is, I can't stop thinking about you. Monica, you've done something to me that I wasn't able to explain before. But I think...I think I got the gist of it now."

She said nothing, but her heart began to kick at her ribcage.

"You know a lot about me. But I don't think you know about what happened with my ex-wife." He looked down at his hat and was quiet for a long time. He cleared his throat again and spoke slowly. Every word crystal clear, as though he were telling his story for the first time. "I was coming up as a bullfighter. Working bigger and better shows. I met Kelly at an event in Red Bluff. She was the daughter of a rancher out there. We were twenty-two. We fell in love fast, got married in Reno. I brought her to Oleander to live with my family. The idea was I'd work the rodeos to help her pay for college. When she was done, I'd come back and take over the ranch. We had it all planned out."

Monica tried to imagine young Dean, madly in love and optimistic about the future. She'd heard rumors, but never the full story. After his marriage ended, he'd left Oleander for good, crisscrossing the country on the pro bull rider circuit, rarely home, not even on Christmas.

"I don't know if it was being away from her friends and family," Dean continued, "but she started to act up while I was away. Ditching classes. Hanging out with a fast crowd. My mother, my father, even my brothers tried to look after her, but she was like smoke. Weren't nothing that could hold her." He shook his head. "I'd come back in the off-season and we'd try to play husband and wife. But we were always arguing. She'd accuse me of running around on her. I'd swear to God that I was never unfaithful to her, but she didn't believe me."

"Did you love her?"

"I did. And I loved the idea of being a husband. Of having a wife." He took a deep breath. "When things got really bad, she convinced me that the problem between us was that we hadn't started a family. So. We started trying for a baby. She got pregnant right away."

Monica's throat tightened. "I didn't know...I didn't know you had kids."

Dean's voice lowered. "I don't."

She was confused. "What?"

"Halfway through the pregnancy, she up and left with the real father of her baby. Colorado somewhere. I was back on the road before the ink on the divorce papers was dry." He rubbed his beard. "I was probably in some buckle bunny's bed the day that little boy was born."

"Dean," she whispered, feeling his heartache as though it were her own. "God, I'm so sorry."

"Sex numbed the pain for a long time. Got a taste for it, as free and easy as it is on the circuit." His temple twitched as his jaw tightened. "Being back in Oleander, I've had to face those memories. That pain. My dad isn't getting any better. And my brother Daniel is the one with the wife and kids now. He runs the ranch. That could've been my life. I'm proud of him, but...there's always a part of me that wonders what would've happened if it'd all worked out the way I'd planned."

She was silent. All the pieces of the puzzle fit together now except for one—the relationship between her and Dean.

"I've done a lot of soul-searching since you left," he said. "For a while, I wondered if the time we spent together wasn't just me trying to numb the pain again. With sex. The thought scared me."

Was he just using me? That can't be true. It was real. It felt *real.* Panic stabbed the pit of her stomach, but Monica forced herself to sit still.

"So," she said calmly, "what's your conclusion?"

Dean leaned forward in the plush armchair to get a better look at Monica. The cloudy sky filled her office with a soft diffusion of light. Her dark skin glowed. She was dressed in a pale gray blouse that showed off her cleavage and a narrow gray skirt that showed off the deep curve of her hips. Her dark hair was piled into a big messy bun. She was wearing black high heel shoes that were open at the toes. Her neat little toenails—red as a toreador's cape—played peekaboo with him. Very distracting.

He blinked slowly, trying to memorize this image of her in case things went south and this gambit turned out to be a great big failure.

"You said to me once," he began, "that the best we can hope to find is beauty in imperfection. In the things that don't turn out right. In the things that are damaged or incomplete. But I don't agree with you. All of our imperfections as a couple, whatever you think they are, form one picture for me. And that picture is perfect. Perfect and beautiful."

He made himself a little ill with all this love talk. But Monica's eyes had gone misty. And every word he'd said was true.

"Princess, I believe in you and me. My family needs me for now, but I'll do anything to make this work. I'll drive up and see you every weekend. I even bought a brand-new truck. You won't have to ride around in my Dad's old dinosaur or in Caleb's monster truck anymore. Ain't that cool?"

She was quiet, so he soldiered on.

"I know I don't have a lot to offer. And you're an earner, so this probably won't impress you. But I've been working as a professional bullfighter for almost twenty years. I've socked all my contest winnings and earnings away. Bo helped me set up an investment portfolio right after I graduated high school. Ain't got no house, no expenses, no debts. Hell, that truck's the first thing I've had in my name for a long, long time. Paid cash for it. Felt good."

"Why are you telling me all this?"

"Because I've been talking with your father."

That got her. She put her hands flat on her desk as if to steady herself. "What do you mean you've been talking with my father?"

He nodded, trying to appear nonchalant even though winning over Monica's family had been the most difficult thing he'd ever done in his entire life. "Yup. Talking, fishing. I took him riding on the ranch. Cool guy, your father."

Her eyebrows rose. "This is surreal."

"Now, I'm not religious," Dean said. "I never have been. But talking to your Dad, I've learned a lot. He even took me to the *gurdwara*. And I've thought about it on my own. If it is important to you, I'll convert."

She was incredulous. "Are you kidding me? *You* would become a Sikh?"

He smiled. "If that's what it takes."

"What it takes...to what?"

Dean put his hat on her desk, stood up and walked to her. His bad leg creaked like an old pirate ship as he got down on one knee. He reached into his pocket. His sister-in-law Georgia had helped him pick out the ring—with lots of opinionated input from Monica's mother.

"Monica Kaur," he said, opening the box. He'd spent the entire drive to Cupertino memorizing what he'd say. He looked up into her beautiful dark eyes, saw his future and the words flew free. "You are brave, fearless and beautiful. I've never met a smarter or sexier woman. I would be honored to spend the rest of my life doing everything I can to make you happy. Will you marry me?"

She said nothing.

Fear narrowing his vision, Dean cleared his throat and brought out the big guns. "I love you. *Meh tenu pyaar karda hai.*"

A tear rolled down her cheek. "Who...who taught you that?"

"Your brother."

Monica didn't just embrace Dean. She *launched* herself at him. When she threw her arms around his neck, he lost his balance and they crashed to the carpet in a heap of limbs and laughter.

The ring—God help him, the ring that had cost him hours in the arena, torn ligaments, sore muscles and gallons upon gallons of bull snot—rolled under her desk, momentarily forgotten.

"Yes," she whispered. "Yes, I'll marry you, Dean. I love you too."

When she kissed him, Dean finally understood something that had been eluding him for years. There was no outrunning the truth. Drinking, brawling, working, even lovemaking couldn't keep the truth away forever.

The only thing to do was face it.

The truth was, he was made to love one woman. This woman. And in loving her, he'd found in himself a man worthy of love.

They spent a long time on the floor getting lost in one another's kisses. When at last they were done, breathless and disheveled, Monica crawled under her desk, retrieved her ring and slipped it on her finger. Dean lay back with his hands behind his head, watching her as she admired it.

"I've got a surprise for you too, MacKinnon," she said.

She lifted the bouquet of poppies on her desk and pulled out her tablet computer.

"Jesus, not that thing again," he said.

"Shush." She lay back down next to him and started it up. She opened an untitled folder and showed him the file. "I've been working on this for a few weeks now. Tell me what you think."

He looked at it. There were some profit and loss tables, a timeline and what looked to be a detailed business plan for some kind of school. "What is this?"

She reached forward and swiped to a logo and design.

He read it aloud. "Walker-MacKinnon Bull Riding and Bullfighting Academy."

"Now this is all in the early stages of development, but I ran some numbers, and I think this is an incredible opportunity for you and Bo," she said excitedly. Dean faked a skeptical expression, but his little gypsy horse trader wasn't deterred. "Before you say yes or no, just let me show you—"

Dean cut her off with a long, passionate kiss that made her go slack beneath him. When he broke the kiss at last, she opened her eyes and blinked at him.

"Just let me show you," she whispered, stroking his chest with a dreamy look in her eyes, "how taking the academy on the road half the year increases your profits by almost thirty-five percent."

"You don't quit, do you?" he asked, smiling.

"I'm bullish," she said. "I think you can appreciate that."

Monica handed in her notice before lunchtime. By three o'clock, she and Dean were on the road back to Oleander in his brand-new truck.

Dean kept one hand on the steering wheel. With his other hand, he stroked her smooth, warm nape. "I know what Kaur means. It means princess."

"Did you know that when you started calling me princess? Back when we first met?" she asked.

"No. Just a coincidence, I guess."

"Why did you start calling me that anyway?"

He grinned at her. "Because you probably wouldn't have liked the other thing I wanted to call you."

Monica smiled to herself and looked out the window. "We don't *have* to be home tonight, do we?"

"No, not really."

She turned back to him. "There are lots of places to stay in Fresno. We're about half an hour away."

"Come to think of it, I am pretty tuckered out." He faked a yawn.

* * *

Their room was on the third floor of yet another anonymous business hotel. Monica wondered if she was developing a fetish for places like these. Every time she saw one, she got wet on flashbacks of Dean and the no-holds-barred way they devoured each other in quiet, air-conditioned rooms just like these.

When he stuck the keycard in the door, she embraced him from behind and gave his rock-solid torso a squeeze.

"Have you been thinking about me?" she whispered.

The light turned green on the lock. "Let's just say my right hand is mighty glad we're back together," he said.

As soon as the door closed behind them, Dean was all over her. Eyes on fire, he ripped her blouse open like some hero in a cheesy romance novel. The buttons flew. As she kicked off her shoes, he unhooked her bra, unzipped her skirt and, in a breathless rush, threw her backwards onto the bed.

He took off his hat and jacket, then stripped off his shirt. His white cotton undershirt strained against his muscular shoulders and chest.

"I've never gone this long without sex, Monica," he said, unbuckling his belt as she gazed up at him. His voice was a low growl resonant with pent-up lust. "I feel like I'm gonna jump out of my skin." He narrowed his eyes at her. "Fuck."

He bent down, grabbed her hips in his big hands and buried his face against her pink lace panties, filling his lungs with her scent. She should've been embarrassed. But with Dean, this was how it was—they were animals in heat, addicted to each other's bodies, high on the hunt.

Quickly, he pulled down her panties and dropped them on the floor. He put his hands on her thighs and spread her legs wide. His eyes feasted on her as he stood up. He began to unbutton his fly. "Touch yourself. Get that pretty pussy ready for me."

Monica reached down between her legs. She ran her middle finger up and down her seam, stopping to dip the pad of her finger in the liquid heat pooling at her opening. As Dean watched her, she spread the slickness all over her pussy lips. They had begun to swell and flare in anticipation of his touch—his fingers, his tongue, his cock.

"Yes." He pulled the undershirt over his head. She never got tired of ogling his beautiful body—scarred, tatted, hairy, muscular, he was a fucking specimen, that Dean MacKinnon. Her walking fantasy. Her wet dream. Her goddamned *fiancé.*

On that thought, she dragged her fingertip over her swollen clit. Her pussy clenched at the sharp spike of pleasure.

He took off his boots, his jeans and his boxers all at once. His monster of a cock sprang up, swollen and dusky. Her mouth watered.

Standing above her, he stared at the finger working her clit.

"You're magnificent," he murmured. He took his cock in his fist and gave himself a single, slow pump. "Spread some of that candy on your nipples for me."

Her clit was already twitching under her trigger finger. She was only a few breaths away from coming. But she stopped fondling herself long enough to plunge her finger back into her hot pussy. She pulled it back out, then spread her juices on each of her hardened nipples like some kind of depraved nymphomaniac, which wasn't too far from the truth when it came to how she acted around Dean.

"Touch that pretty clit again," he ordered. Her hand slid down her stomach and she went back to pleasuring herself, making sure to hold back whenever she got too close to the edge. Dean had taught her that—edging. Orgasm denial. The technique had added nuance and intensity to both their lovemaking and her solo time. But she'd been so long without him that she wasn't sure she'd be able to hold back.

He climbed on top of her, his imposing body curving over hers. Heat poured off his skin. He kissed her—a slow, lingering lover's kiss, restrained but hungry. When he kissed her neck, she closed her eyes. And when his hot lips landed on one of her nipples, she hissed with pleasure so pure, sparks formed behind her eyelids.

He suckled her hard, strumming her nipple with the hardened tip of his tongue. When he released her, the nipple was rosy and erect. Her skin almost hissed when it touched the cool air-conditioned air.

"I missed the taste of your cunt," he murmured against her breast.

He was filthy. She loved it.

Dean gave her other nipple equal treatment, but finished by tugging at her gently with his teeth. She arched her back, the sweet pain tempered by pleasure.

He kissed down her belly, then gently took her hand and moved it away from her pussy.

"My turn."

He stuck his middle and index fingers in his mouth, wet them and pressed them into her soaking heat. He wasn't gentle, but she was so turned on that shock turned to pleasure as he began to fuck her, working against the tight resistance of her body. She was so wet that the room filled with the sound of his fingers sliding in and out. Her nipples tightened even further and her lungs began to draw more air, sending fresh blood to her core.

When his hot lips found her clit, she was already airborne. Three swipes of his tongue and she flew apart at once, the orgasm ripping through her like an exorcism. Her pussy squeezed him but he pushed back, scissoring his fingers and drawing out that first wild climax until she was screaming with pleasure, grabbing at his rock-solid arms like she was about to get swept off the face of the earth.

Before she could come down from her high, Dean pulled his fingers from her, grabbed a condom from the pocket of his jeans, tore it open and rolled it on.

With a grunt, he grabbed her and dragged her to the middle of the bed. He hooked his hands behind her knees and spread her legs as wide as they would go. He leaned forward and fitted his cock at her opening like an archer would nock an arrow. Her pussy, still twitching, began to suck greedily at his cockhead, hungry for more.

"It's going to be a long night, princess," he said.

"I'm counting on it, cowboy," she whispered.

His eyes were like two blue flames in the fading sunlight. Without another word, he flexed his ass and swung his hips forward, slamming her hard against the mattress as he filled her with his cock. He pulled out almost to the tip and thrust again. When he did it once more, a second orgasm grabbed her by surprise. She shut her eyes tight and lost all control. Every muscle below her waist seized up and her pussy detonated in a long string of wet, brutal contractions. She squirted all over him. What had he done to her? She felt shameless, warped and hot as hell.

"Fuck yes," Dean said, laughing and kissing her cheeks. "You fucking goddess."

"What was that?" she whispered when it was over. Her head fell back on the mattress. She was out of breath.

"That's us." He stroked her face.

She looked at the clock. "We've been in this room for ten minutes. How on earth did you make me come twice in ten minutes?"

He gave her a lingering kiss followed by another delicious deep thrust. "The real question," he said with a grin, "is how I made you come three times in fifteen."

"Cocky bastard," she whispered.

* * *

At dawn, Dean tucked the bedsheets around them and brushed Monica's wild black hair away from her beautiful face. She wore nothing except a smile and her engagement ring. Pride swelled in his chest.

She said yes.

Too exhausted to get up and shut the curtains, he watched the sun rise slowly over the Sierra Nevadas. When the bright sun's edge finally broke free from the mountaintops, he pulled Monica close and kissed her lips.

"I love you, Dean," she murmured, half-asleep.

"I love you too."

"I can't believe you came back to me."

"'Course I did, princess." He closed his eyes at last. "You brought me back to life."

This cowboy and cowgirl sell the steak and the sizzle.

Please see the next page for a preview of

Cowboy Player

*I wonder how many people I've looked at all my life
and never seen.*

—JOHN STEINBECK

With a grimace, Melody swallowed down the last of her gin and tonic. One of the bartenders whisked her glass away and asked if she wanted another. Even though she did, Melody shook her head.

Something touched her bare arm. A warm fingertip grazed her skin from elbow to wrist. She looked up.

"Lost in thought again?" Clark leaned close and kissed her cheek, just as he had hundreds of times before. One of the Silver Spur's waitresses put a beer down in front of him and flashed a sexy grin. He smiled at the woman briefly and turned his attention back to Melody.

She shook her head. "It must be hard to be you."

"Why do you say that?"

"Women. The endless parade of women fighting for your attention."

"Oh, it's not so bad." Clark took a sip of beer.

"Where are all your brothers? They usually help carry the burden."

"I'm on my own tonight," he said. "But let's talk about you, not me. Why so blue, Mel? Baby sister all grown up?"

They turned to look at the crowd in front of the stage. Harmony had found herself a cowboy admirer. The lucky fellow was holding her close and nuzzling her neck as he led her around the dance floor.

Was Melody sad that Harmony was growing up? No, not exactly. Nostalgic, more like—for a version of herself she wasn't sure ever existed. Had she ever been that young and optimistic? Had she ever let herself be that free?

"I'm proud of her," Melody said at last. "It's been hard. Seeing our mom get sick like that. Lots of kids would've dropped out. But she finished school with a 3.8. This is her first night out in a long, long time."

"A smarty-pants, just like you."

"Smarter than me," said Melody. "She learned something useful. Solid paycheck, helping others, all that good stuff."

"You're a brilliant teacher, from what I've heard."

"Diagramming sentences isn't exactly going to save us from the zombie apocalypse, now is it?"

"If there's a zombie apocalypse, nothing will save us, Mel. The only thing left to do is get drunk and screw." He held up his beer mug and winked at her. An honest-to-goodness wink.

Melody shook her head. "You can't help yourself, can you, MacKinnon? You're a hopeless flirt."

"Flirting? Thought I was just drinking beer and being myself." He looked down at the empty coaster in front of her. "What about you? What are you having? Gin and tonic, right?"

He remembered her favorite drink. Melody smiled. "No, I'm good. I'm on sister watch tonight. She really wants to cut loose. Someone's gotta hold her hair back when the vomit flies. Which it inevitably will." She waved her hand at him. "You should go have a good time. Get yourself a nice piece. Enjoy your Saturday night."

Only Clark could make a shrug look so sexy. "But I'm already enjoying my Saturday night."

Something about the way he said those words made Melody's skin tingle.

As an experiment, she uncrossed her legs and leaned forward, resting her arms on the bar. For a nanosecond, Clark's dark eyes darted to her cleavage before resting on his beer. A sudden, electric thrill shimmied down her spine. Her body clenched with pleasure, knowing she could still get the attention of a man as insanely hot as Clark MacKinnon.

But then...guilt.

That's Clark. Don't flirt with Clark.

The band started playing something loud and rowdy. Clark leaned forward. As he spoke into her ear, his warm breath caressed the sensitive skin on her neck. "You know, Lucky's going to be doing the rodeo circuit soon. It'll be just you and me on the road. Hours and hours together. You ready for that, Mel?"

Melody cleared her throat. *Be cool. Make a joke. Keep your distance.* "You and me and a couple hundred pounds of raw meat? Sounds kinky, Superman."

In the crowded bar, Clark stood flush against her, his arm pressed against hers. The sleeves of his dark T-shirt molded to the broad muscles in his biceps. Where the cotton ended, his skin was smooth and hot. She'd spent enough time with Clark shut up in the van to know he smelled pretty good—soap and leather, a little drugstore aftershave. Up close was a different story. That familiar smell, mixed with the subtle scent of his skin, made the transmission fall out of Melody's self-control.

"I had a feeling you might be kinky, Santos," he said.

He moved even closer. With gentle fingers, he brushed her long hair away from her neck and tucked the curls behind her ear. Intentionally or not, his bottom lip brushed her earlobe as he whispered, "Am I right?"

Christ. Heat rushed like quicksilver to her core, leaving her fingers and toes tingling with cold. She hadn't been this turned on in months, maybe years. Under the bar, she pressed her thighs together to ease the hot ache that Clark had summoned with nothing more than a few whispered words and the caress of his fingertips.

"Clark, what are you..." She trailed off and looked into his eyes.

Was he teasing her? Was he serious?

She and Clark had played in the creek together as little kids and slammed each other with dodgeballs in the schoolyard. She'd spent years in his company and yet, she couldn't remember what color his eyes were. Here in the neon light, she couldn't see his irises. But she could feel the unfamiliar heat of his gaze burning her like a thousand suns. Coming from a friend or lover, that look meant desire. That look meant sex.

The band finished the song with a loud holler and a wild drum solo. The crowd cheered. Clark locked his eyes on her for a half-second more before Tom Shelton, the big, tough-looking bartender, set down a row of shot glasses on the bar in front of them.

"Hey, Clark. Hey, Mel." Tom proceeded to fill the shot glasses from a bottle of cinnamon-scented whiskey.

Clark blinked and looked up at Tom. Melody folded her hands and rested them on her knees to keep from trembling.

"Your brothers here tonight?" Tom asked Clark.

Clark cleared his throat and shook his head. "No. All of 'em are busy."

"That's a first. How about you? What are you two up to?"

"Just keeping an eye on Mel's little sister."

"No kidding. She's a live wire," said Tom. "These shots are for her group, matter of fact."

Melody leaned back and glanced at the bar where Harmony's friends were sitting, but her little sister wasn't there. Melody looked back at the dance floor. Harmony and her new cowboy friend were nowhere to be seen.

"Clark." She hopped off the barstool. "I've lost sight of my sister. Can you see her?"

A full foot taller than Melody, Clark stood up straight and scanned the crowded room. "She was right there a minute ago."

"Ah, Christ," Melody said.

"We'll find her. She can't have gotten far." Clark grasped Melody's hand in his. With a warm, steady grip, he led her through the crowd, cutting a path for her. Together, they searched the dance floor and the area by the pool tables. They walked down the hallway leading to the restrooms and the smoking patio—still no Harmony. They were almost to the parking lot when Melody saw a flash of glitter in the corner of her eye.

In the darkest corner of the bar, tucked into a booth, Melody's baby sister was straddling a cowboy and sucking his face off like a lamprey on a dead flounder. The cowboy's big hands gripped the backs of Harmony's bare thighs and together they looked like they were doing a very private dance in public.

"What the hell!" Melody exclaimed. "Harmony!"

Harmony popped up, surprised. Her lipstick was smeared across her mouth and one strap of her dress hung off her shoulder. "Holy shit, Mel!" she exclaimed. She looked between Melody and Clark and after a couple of seconds, began to giggle. She was drunk as a skunk. "You two look like you've seen a ghost."

"Yeah, the ghost of my sister's dignity." Melody went over and adjusted Harmony's dress. "Get up. We're going home."

"What? Why?"

"Why? Because drinking is fine. Dancing is fine. Having sex in public? Not fine." Melody grabbed Harmony's wrist and pulled her to her feet.

"Easy now," Clark said softly. He took Harmony's elbow and helped her get her balance.

Melody looked into the dark booth to see who'd taken advantage of her sister. "You've got some nerve. She's wasted. I have a mind to call the cops on you."

The guy held up his hands. "Please don't call the cops." His words were slurred. He was as drunk as Harmony. "I just did what Clark said to do and the next thing I know—"

Melody knocked the hat off the cowboy's head to get a look at his face. "Holy fuck! Lucky!"

He blinked. "I'm so sorry, Melody. We just got carried away."

Behind her, Clark let out a hoot. When Melody glared at him, he pressed his lips together, but his eyes were still laughing. "No harm done, Mel," he said, holding Harmony up as she swayed on her feet. "Come on. Let's get these two train wrecks home."

ALSO BY MIA HOPKINS

The Cowboy Cocktail Series
Cowboy Valentine
Cowboy Resurrection
Cowboy Player
Cowboy Karma
Cowboy Rising

The Kings of California Series
Deep Down
Hollywood Honkytonk

ABOUT THE AUTHOR

Mia Hopkins writes lush romances starring fun, sexy characters who love to get down and dirty. She's a sucker for working class heroes, brainy heroines and wisecracking best friends. She lives in Los Angeles with her roguish husband and waggish dog.

For more information, please visit her website at www.miahopkinsauthor.com.